I0716865

HIS DESTINY

HIS CONFESSION TRILOGY
BOOK 3

ANGEL RAYNE

His Destiny
Copyright © Angel Rayne 2024
All Rights Reserved

This is a work of fiction. Names, characters, places, events, organizations, and incidents are either products of the author's imagination or are used fictitiously. Any resemblance to actual persons, living or dead, or actual events, is purely coincidental.

No part of this book may be reproduced, or stored in a retrieval system, or transmitted in any form or by any means, electronic, mechanical, photocopying, recording, or otherwise without the express written permission of the publisher, except for the use of brief quotations in a book review.

Thank you for respecting the hard work of this author.

Published by Everblood Publishing, LLC
https://everbloodpublishing.com

ISBN- 978-1-945499-84-5

Cover Design by Dar at Wicked Smart Designs

Proofreader: Mackenzie @ NiceGirlNaughtyEdits.com

ALSO BY ANGEL RAYNE

<u>Mafia Romance Reading Order</u>

<u>Luca and Veda</u>

His Game

His Stakes

His Win

<u>Enzo and Sera</u>

His Promise

His Rejection

His Proposal

<u>Tristan and Luna</u>

His Darkness

His Deception

His Destiny

<u>**Stand Alone Novels**</u>

<u>**Tyler and Ailee**</u>

Be With Me

SYNOPSIS

I've always been empty. A void where a soul should be.
Now, everything is different. Because of *her*...

Monsters aren't supposed to have empathy. That's why I
was the perfect mafia enforcer. Cold. Brutal and efficient.

Until I dragged Luna into the dark with me.

Even as my captive, she shined her light into all
the scarred, tortured parts of my world, forcing me to
realize I might be human after all.

And I hate it.

I have no idea what to do with these emotions. Desires.
The overwhelming need I have for her touch, her body,
her soul.

I know I can protect her from our mutual enemy. That's
why I kidnapped her in the first place.

But I'm starting to wonder if *I'm* the one who needs to be
saved. Because for the first time in a long time, maybe
ever, I think I'm...afraid.

After all, what kind of twisted beast will I become now that my heart—the one I only *just* realized I have—is in her delicate hands?

CHAPTER 1

Tristan

I stepped into my office, then stood in the center of the room, not knowing what else to do. An hour had gone by since I'd come home to an empty house, and I still found it hard to breathe. On Luca's orders, his men had searched the grounds while Luca, Enzo, and I went through every corner of his house and mine. We'd checked the security footage. She wasn't here.

It was like she'd vanished into thin air.

My gaze landed on the painting that covered my small wall safe for just a second before sliding away, but then I frowned and gave it a second look. Something was...off. I cocked my head as I studied it, but couldn't immediately pinpoint what was wrong. It was just more of a feeling.

A flicker of unease curled in my gut as I approached it. I kept my demons locked away in that safe—pieces that formed the mosaic of my life's darkest moments. But still, it contained parts of me that certain people weren't ever meant to see unless I chose to show them. And there were very few people I allowed into that part of my life.

Taking the picture off the wall, I set it to the side. The safe door was closed. I wiggled the handle. It was locked, as it should be. Tapping in the code, I pulled it open. Inside, everything was as I'd left it.

I started to close it again, but then I hesitated. Rifling through the papers, I pulled out the stack of pictures and thumbed through them. They were all there—except one.

Taking them to my desk, I sat down and checked them again, just to make sure it wasn't stuck to another photo. Setting the stack aside, I searched the area around my desk, and then the entire office, throwing books to the floor and sending papers and pens flying as my previous unease escalated to panic.

But deep down, I knew I hadn't dropped the photo, because I would never have been so careless. Especially not with that particular photo. I'd left it with the others. I knew I had. Just like I also knew who had it now.

My pulse thundered in my ears.

She knew.

Luna had been here, rifling through the layers of my past without my permission, and she'd found the photo of her and her mother. I didn't know how I was so certain of this fact, I just was.

My heart hammered against my ribcage in a violent staccato before I gave myself an internal shake. I was panicking for no reason. How would she have gotten into the safe? There's no way she would have guessed the code. Unless I'd left it open?

Normally, I would say that wasn't possible. I was meticulous with my privacy. However, the last time I'd been in here was after I'd shown Enzo the photo. I'd left it lying on the kitchen table, and put it back in the safe later. After I'd told her Gino was her biological father. I'd been distracted, my mind on Luna.

If she'd figured out why I'd kept it—if she'd connected the dots as to why I had these photos—this new twisted bond forming between us would snap before it had the chance to strengthen into something more.

My mind spun in circles. Did I want some kind of relationship with her? Was I even capable of such a thing? I didn't know. But I wanted the chance to find out.

"LUNA!" I screamed her name, even though I knew she wouldn't answer. My voice echoed off the walls, mocking me, reminding me that I was alone. Always alone.

It'd never bothered me before. As a matter of fact, I preferred the silence of solitude. At least I had, until

Luna had stumbled into my life. But within the weeks I'd known her, it was getting harder and harder to remember my life before her. And try as I might to keep them at bay, scenarios about where she was and who she was with raced through my mind, each one more horrifying than the last.

The silence mocked me as I stormed through the house, searching—*again*—for some kind of clue as to where she went, every step laden with dread that I would find nothing. That she'd somehow just vanished into thin air.

Or worse, that she'd never been here to begin with and had only been a sick figment of my imagination. Something my mind made up just to fuck with me. As if the nightmares and the memories of my childhood weren't torture enough.

I stopped suddenly in the middle of the hallway. Was it true? Had I finally lost my mind completely?

But no. It couldn't be. Pressing my fingers to my temples, I closed my eyes. I could still feel the silky texture of her hair and the softness of her skin. Her clothes were in my fucking bedroom, her toiletries were in my bathroom, and the scent of sex still lingered on my sheets.

I could still taste her on my tongue.

The two men I considered my friends, or at least as much as I was capable of, knew she was here. Luca—the fucking mafia boss—had seen her. Enzo had talked to her.

Taken care of her when I was too much of a coward to show my face. If she wasn't real, if I was starting to hallucinate, he wouldn't have played along. He would've told Luca, who would've thrown me in a fucking psych ward somewhere.

I took a deep breath and tried to get my shit together. Luna was gone. Now, I needed to figure out where the fuck she was. She couldn't have gone far. All our vehicles were accounted for, and none of the guards had seen her leave. It was the middle of the day, and cameras covered every inch of Luca's property. There were no blind spots. No way she could've snuck past them on foot without being seen.

Back in the living room, shards of sunlight cut through the blinds. I closed them so violently that one came loose and fell to the floor with a clatter. But it made no difference. There was no light in this house. Not now. Not without Luna.

I cursed under my breath and strode to the kitchen. It was spotless, as always—except for her clean dishes drying in the sink. So she'd eaten the breakfast I'd left her, and then...what?

Again, I forced myself to stop and take a breath. Perhaps I was wrong and, in my distracted state, the photo had merely been misplaced somehow. In that case, I was panicking about nothing.

She was close to her brother and spoke to him often. It was possible she'd caught a ride to see him. Called an Uber or something, and by some miracle made it to the front gate without being seen. But why would she leave without telling me after promising she would stay in the house?

The answer, of course, was simple. Because she knew I wouldn't let her go, and she'd taken the first chance she'd gotten to leave.

I rubbed my temples with my fingertips. No. No matter what I tried to tell myself, deep down in my black soul, I knew that wasn't the only reason.

She *knew*. I felt the certainty of this all the way down to my bones. She'd figured out my secret and finally saw me for the monster I truly was. Not because of my scars or the abuse inflicted upon me. But because of what *I'd* done.

Shadows encroached on the edges of my vision and my palms grew clammy. How could she ever forgive me?

What if she never did?

Inhaling deep, I realized it didn't matter. I was no hero, and I'd never claimed to be one. I'd never pretended to be anything but what I am. But if there was one truth I couldn't deny, it was that Luna had seeped into the cracks of my cold heart, and now that I knew what it was to be with her, I would do whatever had to be done to get her back. I didn't care if she forgave me or not. Eventually, she'd learn to live with what I'd done.

She was mine now, and I wouldn't—I *couldn't*—let her go.

CHAPTER 2

Tristan

My cell phone vibrated in my coat pocket. "Yes?" I snapped without looking at the screen.

"She's not at her brother's," Matteo told me, and I closed my eyes as something heavy settled in my gut. If Luna had shown up anywhere near that college campus, he would've found her. He was one of my most trusted—and discreet—contacts and I paid him well to remain so. "He hasn't been to any of his classes all morning, so I went to his dorm room. Neither of them was there. No one's seen her or her brother anywhere around the building since yesterday."

I stilled, my blood running cold as my worst imaginings became real. "Were Logan's things in his room?"

"Yes. Everything was there. His roommate told me he hasn't seen Logan since last night when they were hanging out. He got a strange phone call in the middle of a video game and Logan went out into the hall to speak to whoever it was. He said he seemed off when he came back into their room. Logan told him he was meeting someone for a late dinner and left shortly after. He wouldn't tell him who it was that called, and he hasn't seen him since. The school's camera footage only showed him walking away from his dorm and getting into a black sedan. There was no sign of Luna anywhere."

I didn't ask him how he'd gotten a hold of the camera feeds. I didn't need to. Matteo was damn good at his job. And if he said she wasn't there, I believed him. "What did the car look like?"

"Black, as I said. Nondescript. Dark windows. I couldn't get a read on the plates. The video feed was too blurry to make out the numbers."

"Thank you," I told him. "I appreciate your time."

Grabbing a screwdriver from one of the kitchen drawers, I strode to my bedroom and entered the walk-in closet. Carefully, so as not to leave any telltale marks, I pried up a few of the floorboards and set them aside so I could access the safe hidden underneath. My thumbprint opened the door, and I took stock of the weapons and ammo I kept hidden there. It would do.

Retrieving a black duffle bag from the top shelf above me, I loaded everything into it except for one pistol. Taking the bag and the gun to my bed, I quickly changed out of my suit before stashing a box of ammo into the outside thigh pocket of my tactical pants and sliding one of my favorite knives into my left boot. Then I holstered the pistol at my side as I reviewed what I knew so far.

Luna and Logan were both missing. Luna would do anything for her brother. Hell, she'd sold herself to Gino to take care of him. I also knew Gino would have someone watching Logan, and if she'd snuck out to see her brother, he would've grabbed her before she got anywhere near him.

Gino suspected that I'd taken Luna, but he had no way of proving it.

Still, my gut told me that if I found Gino, I'd find her. And probably her brother, too. He'd likely used Logan to lure her away from the safety of Luca's compound. And instead of coming to me for help, she'd left to deal with it on her own. Just like the stubborn, infuriating woman she was.

Enzo was leaning casually against the side of my house with his arms crossed over his chest when I walked out the front door. I barely gave him a glance.

"Where are you going, T?"

"Where do you think?" Opening the passenger side door of the SUV, I threw the duffle bag inside and slammed the door closed. As I walked around the front of the vehicle, he met me at the driver's side door. I leveled a look at him. "What."

He took my impatience in stride. "Luca told me Luna is gone."

I stared at him and said nothing.

"Do you know where she went?"

"No."

"Do you know why she left?"

"No." Recognizing the lie for what it was, I shook my head and tried again as I got into the SUV. "Yes." That didn't quite feel right either. "Maybe."

"Tristan." Stepping in the way of the door so I couldn't close it in his face, he braced his other arm on the doorframe. "I know what you're doing."

"Do you." It wasn't a question.

"Luca's had men watching Gino's house. We don't know where he is."

"I'll find him."

He stared at me hard for a moment. "You really think he has her again."

There was no sense in lying to him about it. "Yes."

Enzo shook his head, his jaw clenched so hard he spoke through his teeth. "This is reckless, even for you. You can't go after Gino by yourself. Let me call Luca and have him call for reinforcements. We'll come with you, and we'll find Luna together."

I grabbed the door handle, about to slam the door with him in it if necessary. There wasn't time for Luca to organize a search party. But at the last minute, I stopped.

"What?" he asked. Through the dark lenses of his glasses, I felt him studying my face. "What is it, T?"

I couldn't bring myself to look at him as I asked, "She was real, right?"

His eyebrows furrowed in confusion. "What do you mean?"

I glanced in his direction, but didn't have the balls to see the truth in his expression and looked away again. Still, I needed to know. "She was really here? You're not just playing along with some psychotic break I'm having or something?"

Taking off his glasses so I could see the sincerity in his eyes, he said, "Yes. Luna was...*is* real, Tristan."

I nodded as some of the stiffness left my shoulders. "I have to go."

"Come on," he said as he put his glasses back on. "Wait. At least give me a minute to grab more weapons and let Luca know what's going on and I'll come with you."

I shook my head. "I don't want your help, Enzo. This is between me and Gino, and you don't need to get dragged into it. Now get the fuck out of the way, because I really don't want to hurt you."

After a moment, he stepped back. "If you're not back in two hours, I'm coming after you."

Without looking at him again, I shut the door and drove off.

The drive to Gino's was a blur. I didn't have a plan, and I didn't need one. All I knew was that I would tear that place apart brick by brick if I had to in order to find any clue as to Luna's whereabouts. My fingers tightened on the wheel as adrenaline coursed through my veins, and more than once I had to remind myself to watch my speed. A dead cop was a little harder to make disappear than a civilian corpse. Not impossible, but I didn't have time right now to deal with that shit.

When I arrived at Gino's property, the gate was closed. I started to drive past to my usual parking spot up the road, but slammed on the brakes and threw the car into reverse. I swung the SUV around and lined up the front end with the gate. My upper lip lifted in disgust as I stared at the home of the *bastardo* who had made my childhood—and now my adult life, and Luna's—a living hell.

My pulse pounded in my ears, drowning out the echoes of my childhood screams as memories circled around me like vultures, waiting for me to succumb so they could pluck out my entrails.

Something had been unleashed within me the night he'd caught me in Luna's room and forced me down into that cold basement. He'd taken my innocence. My childhood. Taken *everything*. But he wasn't going to take Luna from me. This time, I wasn't hiding in my cell. This time, I wasn't locking the monster back into the box where I kept all the dark things within me.

An icy calm settled over me, and I stomped my foot down on the gas pedal and slammed through the gate, flying up the winding driveway right to the house. My tires spit up gravel as I skidded to a halt outside the front steps. Grabbing the duffel bag from the passenger seat, I left the car door open for a quick escape and strode up to the double doors. Without pausing, I kicked them open, my pistol raised and ready.

"GINO!" His name roared from deep within my chest, echoing through the halls as I waited for a response. Only silence greeted me. Slinging the duffel bag over my shoulder, I quickly cleared the rooms closest to me, finding no one. The house appeared deserted, as Enzo said.

As I made my way back toward the kitchen, I stopped in front of a closed door. Watched my hand as it reached for the knob, turned it, and pulled. It swung open with a soft creak. A set of wooden stairs led down into the darkness.

I stood frozen, the fingertips of my left hand rubbing against my palm, feeling the phantom texture of each step as I'd crawled up them to escape the horrors below. No one was down there, or I would've felt the burn of a bullet by now. Yet I couldn't stop my hand from shaking as I flicked on the light.

One foot at a time, I forced myself down the steps, if for no other reason than to prove that I could. That he hadn't broken me completely. Not yet.

When I reached the bottom, I stopped, my eyes on the cement floor. It was as far as I could make myself go. I smelled leather and the tangy, metallic scent of the chains that hung from the ceiling. The acrid sting of bleach burned my nostrils and made my eyes water. My stomach rolled and my heart rate spiked as my muscles tensed in preparation to fight. Or perhaps, run. At that moment, I couldn't have said which.

My eyes felt impossibly heavy as I lifted my gaze from the floor. The leather couch looked exactly as I remembered, the chains still hung from the ceiling, and the cement floor was stained with the remnants of blood from the men I'd killed.

The bodies, of course, were no longer there. Milo had come to collect them, and he was damn good at his job. It would be impossible to collect any DNA evidence from the scene.

A cold sweat dripped into my eyes, and I swiped it away with the back of my hand. I wanted to run back up the stairs and burn this entire house to the fucking ground, but I forced myself to stand there.

Then I stayed for another few minutes. I didn't move. Screams rang in my ears, mostly my own. And my skin crawled with the memory of hands all over my body, stripping off my clothes. Touching me. Touching me everywhere...

I closed my eyes again and rode it out. Only when the screams faded and there was silence again did I allow myself to go back upstairs and down the second hallway.

My gaze landed on Gino's office door. If there was anything in this house that would lead me to his whereabouts, that's where I would find it. I tested the handle and found it locked. Taking a step back, I kicked in the door, the wood splintering around the lock with a satisfying sound, then immediately flattened my back against the wall.

Pistol at the ready, I bent down to make myself a smaller target and stuck my head around the frame, quickly scanning the room. Assured no one was in there, I straightened and stepped inside, looking around with mild curiosity. His heavy wooden desk sat front and center, buried under notebooks and loose sheets of paper. Gino had never trusted technology as long as I'd known him. He was old school. And if he'd made a leap into the future recently and gotten a computer or a laptop, it wasn't here. A built-in bookshelf lined the wall to my left, and a large fireplace took up the wall to my right, flanked by ugly paintings of Jesus on one side and the Virgin Mary on the other. Rosary beads and an old Bible laid on the mantel.

Was this where he prayed for his soul after he raped his daughter?

Crossing to the desk, I holstered my gun, picked up a notebook, and started flipping through the pages. It appeared to be a log of all the business transactions he took care of for Luca. Setting it to the side, I rifled through the stack of papers and found a collection of bizarre notes. Mostly what appeared to be drunken ramblings to his dead wife.

A corner of a piece of paper stuck out from the middle of another pile. The word *"Perdonami"*—forgive me—was written in a dark scrawl across the top. I pulled it out and scanned the rest of the letter, feeling absolutely nothing as I read the mental breakdown of a man who utterly deserved it. It was a suicide note dated the night I took Luna from here. Whose forgiveness was he asking for? Luna's? Or God's? It certainly wasn't mine.

I crumbled the note into a ball and threw it on the floor, then continued searching, but I found nothing to indicate where Gino might be hiding out. Gathering up the notebooks, I stuffed them into the duffel bag to take back to Luca.

Picking up my bag, I glanced around one last time, clenching my fists in frustration. Luna was out there somewhere, scared and alone. And it was all because of me.

Because I was a fool.

She'd convinced me to let her out of the cell. That she wouldn't leave. I thought she'd understood I only wanted to keep her safe. I thought I could trust her.

I thought...I thought...

Something cracked inside my chest, the pain so intense I fell back against the wall and slowly slid down to land hard on the cold tile floor. The duffel slipped from my grip and fell to the floor beside me.

I thought she wanted to stay with me.

Was I that stupid? So desperate for human connection that I believed Luna cared for me? Was it all just an act? If so, she was a very good actress, and she'd made a complete and utter fool out of me.

I rested my elbows on my knees and dropped my head into my hands. My actions had caused her pain and confusion. I'd seen it on her face and in her eyes. And it was why she hadn't trusted me enough to come to me. To let me help her. And now my carelessness may have put her directly in harm's way.

My chest tightened until I could barely draw a breath. If anything happened to her out there, if Gino hurt her again, I would never forgive myself.

I slammed my fist into my forehead. What the fuck was happening to me? This beautiful, maddening, confusing woman made me feel weak. Helpless.

And yet...more of a man than I ever have in my life.

Taking a deep breath, I lifted my head, finally admitting to myself there was nothing I could do right now. I had no idea where to fucking start looking for her. Yet, I wasn't giving up. Luna needed me, and I would move heaven and earth to find her.

Because I needed her even more.

CHAPTER 3

Luna

Earlier That Day

I clutched my phone way too tight as I stared at the cryptic message from my little brother.

> How many other secrets have you kept
> from me, Luna?

THE TEXT WAS SO COLD, so unlike Logan. He never called me Luna. He always called me Luni. Always. My heartbeat pounded in my ears as I read it again and again, trying to make sense of it, but knowing there was only one scenario that would have him sending me a text like this.

Logan found out something. But what? And how? There were a lot of things I'd kept from my brother. Mostly for his own protection, and some just because he didn't need to know. All of which would only cause him pain, or, at the very least, change the way he looked at me.

And I think that was what I was most afraid of.

Instead of texting him back, I called his number with shaky fingers. It rang three times before the call was answered, but it wasn't my brother on the other end.

"That didn't take you long at all."

Fear twisted my bowels as Gino's overly friendly voice greeted me. "Why do you have Logan's phone? Where's my brother?" I demanded. "Let me talk to him. Right now!"

Gino chuckled. "Patience. *Patience,* Luna. He's right here. My long-lost son." He drew the words out sarcastically.

I heard a slap and Logan's answering grunt of pain. Anger and fear warred within me, making my hands tremble. "If you fucking hurt him, Gino, I swear to fucking god—"

He cut me off. "I've been telling him all about our recent re-acquaintance, and what a *whore* his sister is."

Oh, god. Oh god. My stomach churned and bile rose in my throat. "It's true then." I had to force the words out. "You really are my father, and you've known all along."

I knew he was deliberately trying to provoke me, toying with my emotions by insulting and degrading me. But I also had no doubt in my mind that he'd done exactly as he'd just said. I swallowed hard, clenching my jaw as I fought to steady my breathing. I wouldn't let Gino have the satisfaction of knowing how deeply his words had cut me. Not because I'd fucked him without knowing who he was, but because this was one of those things I never wanted Logan to know.

"Of course, I knew. Why do you think I allowed you in on the poker game, Luna?"

"What kind of disgusting piece of shit fucks his own daughter?"

He was silent on the other end of the line for so long I thought he'd hung up. "Hello? Hello? Gino!"

"At first, he tried to defend you," he said quietly. "But when I laid the cards out on the table—so to speak—well, let's just say he knows now that you've been lying to him all along."

Gino's mocking tone made my blood boil even as a shiver of dread crept up my spine. What else had he told Logan about me? How much did he know?

I gave myself an internal shake. It didn't matter. What was important right now was getting him away from Gino and somewhere safe. "Where do you have my brother?"

He didn't answer.

"Gino! Where the fuck is my brother?"

"Meet us at the construction site on East 7th," Gino told me. "I think you're right. It's time for a little family reunion. And Luna..." There was a long pause. "Be sure to come alone." He inhaled loudly through his nose, his voice dropping. "I loved your mother, and when she had you, a girl in her exact image, it made my heart swell with joy. But I never cared about having a son. Never wanted some kid growing up and thinking he could take what I've worked so hard to achieve. That it was owed to him just because he came from my cock. It would be no hardship for me to make him disappear again, only this time for good. Do you understand?"

The line went dead before I could answer. Horrified panic rose in my chest as I lowered the phone to my side and stood there staring at the open safe in disbelief. Gino had Logan. Logan was in danger because of me. I'd been so caught up in Tristan and our relationship...distracted by what was happening with me...

God, it was so fucking stupid of me not to see this coming.

Gino knew how much Logan meant to me. Of course, he'd go after him to get to me. Because he knew I'd come running to rescue him.

And he was right.

The thought crossed my mind to call Tristan. But then I looked down at the faded picture of me and my mother I still held in my other hand. My chest hollowed out and my throat was thick with tears as I slid it into the back pocket of my jeans. I returned the rest of the photos to the safe I'd found them and closed the door, then hit the lock button. Hanging the painting back where it was, I ran to get my shoes.

I couldn't call Tristan in any case. Gino's warning was quite clear. If I didn't come alone, he'd kill Logan. If I could distract him, there might be a chance I could get my brother somewhere safe.

It wasn't until I stepped outside that I realized I had no idea how I was going to get there. Running back into the house, I searched for the keys to the SUV but couldn't find them anywhere.

"Dammit!"

Frantic now, I ran back outside just in time to see a car coming from Luca's. I hesitated for half a second, then ran out to the main drive, flagging down the driver. I had no idea who was behind the wheel, but I'd have to take the chance it wasn't Tristan or one of the other guys. When the car slowed down, I rushed to the passenger side door as the back window rolled down.

"Luna! What's wrong?" Luca's woman, Veda, was in the backseat. I didn't know if she was aware of my situation with Tristan or if she was surprised to see me at his house, and at the moment, I didn't care. I was just grateful to see her and a driver I'd never met before. If anything, another woman might be easier to convince to help me. And as it turned out, it took no convincing at all.

"I need a ride," I told her. "Please! I need to get to my brother as fast as possible!"

"Of course!" Waving me to the back seat, she moved over for me.

Getting in, I slammed the door shut and wrestled with the seatbelt. My hands were shaking so hard it took me a few tries before I could get it fastened. "I need to go downtown to 7th street."

"Go!" Veda told the driver.

But he was pulling up his phone on the touchscreen on the dash. "I just need to tell Mr. Morelli we're making a stop."

I threw her a panicked look.

"No," she told him firmly. "We don't. Hang up now and just drive. He knows I'm going downtown anyway. It'll just be a quick stop." Gesturing with her hands, she told him, "Go! Or I'll tell him it was you who made us late if anything happens to either of us."

With an unhappy look, he put the car in motion.

Then she turned to me. "Is your brother okay?"

"I don't know," I told her honestly, then added a half-lie. "I got a strange text from him and now he's not answering me."

"Go faster," she told the driver when we hit the road. "But don't get pulled over. I'll call Luca and explain everything once we get her there."

I didn't know if she would really tell him or not, but I didn't tell her not to, because I was fucking terrified. I had no idea what I was about to walk into, and if she called Luca after they dropped me off, Tristan would come for me. I completely believed that, because he told me he always would.

With a quick glance at the driver, I whispered, "I was told to come alone." I didn't want to say more than that, but I hoped it would be enough to let Tristan know to be careful. And hopefully, we'd both still be alive when he showed up. I'd ask him about my mother's picture once we were safe.

Veda's eyes widened for a fraction of a second, and then she squeezed my hand to let me know she'd heard me. She didn't let go, holding it the entire trip. I appreciated that she didn't force me to say any more or tell me everything was going to be okay. Instead, she just offered her silent support.

The neighborhood we drove through blurred past the window in a frenzy of winter grays and browns, but I barely noticed any of it. All I could think about was getting to Logan. He was my only real family, and I'd do anything—*anything*—to protect him now. Even if it meant going back to Gino, if that was what he wanted.

I told the driver to drop me off on the corner and I'd walk the rest of the way so Veda wouldn't be late to her appointment, telling her I needed to walk off my panic before I saw him so I didn't come across as a crazy, overprotective sister when it turned out to be nothing. She knew what I was doing, and she didn't want to do it, but I finally got her to agree only when I took her number and promised to call if I needed her to come back.

Waving as they pulled away, I waited until the car was swallowed up by traffic before I turned and ran down the street toward the large construction site I could see two or three blocks ahead.

I slowed down as I approached, catching my breath and scanning the area for any signs of Gino or Logan. Other than the sounds of cars, it was eerily quiet as I ducked under the chain stretched across the entrance to the lot and headed toward the half-built concrete warehouse in the center, my hand up to block the bright sun. But it was still winter, and the wind was really blowing. I wished I'd remembered my coat.

"Logan!" I shouted as I neared. "Logan, where are you?" Fear and panic made my voice abnormally high. I didn't think about being cautious. I didn't give a fuck who heard me. It's not like they didn't know I was coming, and I just wanted to see my brother and make sure he was all right.

I found an unfinished doorway and picked my way over some rocks to get inside. Once I was out of the wind, I turned in frantic circles, searching the cavernous room for any sign of my brother or Gino. "Logan!" Birds flew from the rafters, startling me, and I watched them fly out through a hole where the roof should've been as I tried to get my heart to beat again.

A muffled shout sounded from my right. I hurried toward it, my sneakers slipping on the dusty concrete floor. Behind a stack of steel beams, Logan was bound and gagged, his one unswollen eye dazed with pain and fear. Blood ran down the side of his face from a wide gash in his forehead, dripping onto his white T-shirt, and one of his arms was twisted at a grotesque angle.

I dropped to my knees and pulled the gag from his mouth, then started fumbling with the ropes around his ankles, crying out when he jerked and moaned in pain. "I'm so sorry," I told him as tears blurred my vision. "I'm so, so sorry, honey."

"Luni," he gasped. His speech was slurred, and he spit blood onto the floor. "Get the fuck out of here. Before they come back."

"I'm not leaving you," I choked out. "Can you walk?" I didn't want to move his arm any more than I had to, so I left his hands tied in front of him for now.

His one good eye darted over my shoulder and he opened his mouth to try to warn me. But before I could turn, a massive force slammed into me from behind, catching me on my head and shoulder and throwing me to the side. Stars danced in front of my eyes as the left side of my face scraped along the gritty floor and a heavy weight pinned me down between my shoulder blades. I thrashed violently as I tried to get up, but a hand fisted in my hair, yanking my head back painfully.

Gino's cold voice hissed in my ear. "Welcome back, Luna. It's so good to have the family back together again."

His knee ground into my back as I screamed in rage and frustration. But it was no use. We were trapped. And Gino had won.

CHAPTER 4

Tristan

The sun glinted off the hood of my black SUV, blinding me as I sped toward the spot where Veda said Luna had been dropped off.

It'd been more than twenty minutes since her call, and her panicked voice still rang in my ears. "Tristan? A woman came out of your house as I was driving past. Um, Luna?"

"You saw Luna?"

"Yeah."

My heart began to pound. "Where is she now, Veda?"

She paused, but only briefly. "Look. I don't know what she was doing at your house, but since she seemed unharmed, I'll go ahead and tell you." Veda's fear of me was something I was well aware of, and I forced myself to be patient as she paused again, even though I wanted to jump through the fucking phone and strangle the words out of her. "She said her brother needed her, and she made sure to tell me she was told to come alone. I think something very bad is happening, and I was going to call Luca first, but since she was at your house..."

"Thank you for calling me," I told her. "What else did she say?"

After listening to everything Luna had said on their ride downtown, which wasn't much, I'd jumped up off the floor, grabbed my duffle bag, and ran out of Gino's house.

My hands gripped the steering wheel so hard my fingers were beginning to ache. I didn't need to hear anything else to know who had Luna. I should have foreseen that Gino would go after her brother as a way to draw her out. I should've had someone protecting him, if only to keep her safe.

My stomach churned with unease as I merged into downtown traffic. Gino was ruthless and unpredictable on a good day. When he was desperate, there was no telling what he'd do. And he was desperate right now. Not only to have his daughter back, but because he was in hiding.

What seemed like hours later, I turned sharply onto 7th street. Veda hadn't known exactly where Luna was going, but I could see a construction site ahead. That had to be it. Gino had some fucking balls, calling her out here in the middle of the fucking day. Or maybe he was a genius. With everyone rushing around to and from their downtown jobs, and homeless people rampant in the city now, one lone woman walking down the street would hardly be noticed.

I drove past the site, searching for Gino and the men he doubtless scraped up out of the gutter to work for him, but there were no vehicles or any signs of life. It appeared abandoned, and I started to second guess myself. Driving on, I scanned the area for anywhere else she would've gone, but there was nothing except some houses and a few small businesses. She could be in one of those, but something told me she wasn't.

Circling around, I returned to the construction site and parked in a lot right next door. I picked my bag up off the floor and put it on the passenger seat. I couldn't walk down the street here with an artillery of weapons, so I grabbed one extra Glock and checked the magazine. I checked for cameras and witnesses as I got out of the SUV, then took off my holster and pulled my shirt loose from my pants before hiding that weapon in the back of my waistband so as not to draw any unwanted attention. I slid the smaller weapon into an outside thigh pocket, along with a rag I had in the bag to disguise its shape.

Lastly, I grabbed my favorite knife and tucked it inside the sleeve of my shirt along my inner forearm. Then I stuck two grenades in my front pockets, along with a couple of smoke bombs.

I left the rest of the weapons and ammo in the duffle and put it in the back where the tinted windows would hide the bag from view. Then I hid the keys under the floor mat and left the doors unlocked. I didn't have much of a plan, and the odds were good we'd need to make a quick escape.

The wind whipped around me as I circled the construction site on foot, but I barely felt it. All my focus was concentrated on the sights and sounds around me, and trying not getting killed before I could find Luna. Finding her and getting her to safety was my only priority.

Once I got close enough to the warehouse, I pulled the gun out of my waistband and held it close to the outside of my thigh so it wouldn't be visible from the street. Keeping my eyes and ears open for an attack, I crept around the corner to the back of the building, hoping to find a less obvious way in.

I found a back window that was covered with a weather battered sheet of plastic. It hung in thick shreds and gave me an entry option. Slow and easy, I snuck up to it, angling my body to peer inside. The building was just one big empty room, with only a pile of steel beams to my left. Two guys in suits stood near an open doorway opposite me, and another stood to the right, watching something at the other end of the room. I didn't recognize any of them. And they weren't Italian. The *bastardo* was either getting way too cocky, or he was having trouble finding men who would go along with his ideas.

Taking a moment, I pressed my back against the wall and tried to calm my pulse. I didn't see any signs of Luna, but she had to be in there. I could fucking feel her. Closing my eyes, I steadied my breathing and reached deep inside, finding the cold-blooded machine I was before she'd turned everything upside down. I needed to be calm and logical, or I wouldn't live long enough to save her.

When my blood cooled and my heart slowed to a strong, steady rhythm, I wrapped the rag from my pocket around my head to cover my mouth and nose. Then I pulled the ring from a grenade and tossed it through the ripped plastic to the right, away from anywhere Gino could be hiding Luna and her brother. She would never forgive me if I took him from her, too. Crouching down, I covered my ears and waited for the explosion. Someone screamed. Then I hurled the other one in the same general direction. The screams were cut off and joined by another.

In the chaos that ensued, I pulled the ring from a smoke bomb and threw it inside, waiting a few seconds for the black smoke to cover my entrance before I tore down the plastic and lifted myself up and through the window opening and into the warehouse.

Once inside, I immediately crouched and ran left toward the steel beams, trailing my hand along the wall to guide me. Something on the floor had caught fire from one of the grenades, and the strong stench of chemicals mixed with the smoke, making my eyes water. When I reached the edge of the cloud of smoke, I threw the remaining smoke bomb and swapped my gun to my right hand, pulling my knife with my left.

Gino shouted orders, and I heard the pounding footsteps of his men as they searched for me. A shot rang out. Then another. More shots fired, sounding from all directions. I didn't so much as flinch as a bullet skimmed by my head, burning a trail right above my ear. Every cell in my body was focused on getting to Luna.

The air was thick with the acrid smell of smoke, even through my face covering, making it impossible to see a damn fucking thing. Halfway to the beams, I heard a cough directly behind me and spun around, arcing my knife through the air and smiling when it struck flesh and muscle. Bracing my boot on the body, I yanked the blade free and heard the thud of a body hit the cement floor.

I kept moving, leaving the wall now and continuing toward the pile of beams. The smoke was dissipating, allowing me to see some movement. A guard stumbled in front of me, half of his face and one of his arms missing. I raised my gun and fired. His head lifted in surprise when my bullet slammed into his gut, and his bloodshot eyes locked on mine. I still didn't recognize him. Not that it would matter if I did. He didn't deserve any sympathy from me as he fell to the floor.

Stepping over the body, I watched for the other guard through the thinning smoke and finally spotted him—or what was left of him—scattered on the cement floor.

"Stop right there, Tristan. Or I swear on my God, I'll kill them both."

Abruptly, I froze, gripping my weapons tighter as Gino stepped into view. He held Luna by her long, beautiful hair, and he had a gun to her head. One side of her face was scraped and swollen, and her wide blue eyes were filled with tears and horror as they found mine.

Rage I could no longer control coursed through my veins, bringing with it an icy calm that settled over me like an old friend.

Without hesitation, I raised my gun and fired, hitting Gino in the shoulder.

Luna screamed as the barrel of his gun jerked against her head, but didn't go off. Still, he didn't release her. Instead, he shoved her in front of him like the fucking coward he was.

"Luni? Luna!"

I cocked my head, my eyes never leaving Luna and Gino. The brother, I assumed. He didn't sound good. His voice sounded wet, filled with fluid. Blood, if I had to guess.

"I'm okay," she yelled. "I'm okay."

"You think a bullet will stop me, boy?" Gino suddenly laughed, a deep maniacal sound. "I've survived much more than that, and I'll be here long after you're dead."

"Because you hide behind women?" I taunted. I wanted nothing more than to shoot him in the head, but I couldn't get a clear shot with him holding Luna in front of him. There was too much of a chance he'd move and I'd hit her instead.

Tired of the games, I strode forward to get a closer shot. Gino's eyes widened as he watched me coming for him. He backed up, dragging Luna along until we were all behind the pile of beams.

A young man with the same dark hair as Luna sat on one knee behind Gino and Luna. His wrists were bound and blood dripped from a gash on his head. The eye that wasn't swollen shut went from his sister to me and back again. "Who the hell is that?"

Luna's voice was abnormally high and tinged with fear as she stared at me with conflicted blue eyes. "I think he's my boyfriend..."

Her words hit me hard, stealing my breath, and I felt my entire world shift on its axis.

Boyfriend?

Hearing her claim me in the midst of all of this chaos and violence lit a flicker of warmth in my battered soul. But it was a mundane term. One that didn't come close to describing this thing between us. Luna was a beacon in my dark world. She brought color into my grayscale existence.

No, boyfriend wasn't the right word to describe what we were. It was something much deeper than that.

Gino growled at her response and tightened his grip in her hair, making her wince. "He's not your anything, girl. Do you hear me?" he yelled in her ear. "That"—his voice dripped with disgust as he jerked his chin in my direction—"isn't even a man. He could never love you, *mia figlia.*" My daughter. "Not like I do." He stared directly into my eyes, his features twisting in pain from the gunshot wound I'd given him. "No. He doesn't know what love is. He only knows strength and power. And right now, I'm the one with the power."

He waited for a reaction from me, and I could see his patience waning when he didn't get one. But his words had stopped affecting me a long time ago. There was no way I could've survived being around him all these years if he still held that power over me. And I wasn't in chains now. He could say whatever the fuck he wanted to me, if it would take his attention from his daughter long enough for me to get her the hell out of here.

My eyes went to Luna, and I watched as what little hope she had faded from her face and her shoulders slumped in defeat.

I shook my head. "Don't do that," I told her quietly. "It's not over. Not yet."

Misinterpreting me, Gino scoffed. "That's where you're wrong, boy."

"What are you going to do?" I asked him, genuinely curious. "Shoot her? Her brother? Kill your own children?"

"Yes."

"Why?"

His eyes were wild. "Because I want to see if it will make you feel something."

Luna sucked in a breath, her eyes locking onto mine. I could see her trembling from where I stood. See how afraid she was. And I knew it wasn't just for herself, but for her younger brother who was using the wall against his back for balance as he struggled to get to his feet.

But none of that was what caught and held my attention. There was something in Gino's voice that might give someone else a twinge of hope...regret, maybe? Sadness? But I knew him better than that. I heard the conviction that far overpowered anything else.

I knew Gino's dark side. Maybe better than he knew himself. And I realized then that although she reminded him of his dead wife, Luna was too easy. She'd never given him the sense of conquest he craved, that feeling of power he'd just mentioned. He craved her love...no.

That wasn't right. He craved the love of her mother, and a part of him knew Luna was only a sad substitute. There was only guilt where she was concerned. Whereas he felt no guilt over raping me. As a matter of fact, in some sick, demented way, it did make him feel...powerful.

Lowering the gun to my side, I said, "Take me." Dropping both of my weapons to the floor, I kicked them both toward Gino. Then I pulled the other one from my pocket and tossed that toward him too. "Let them go and take me."

"Tristan, NO!" Luna started to struggle against her father.

"Let her go!" her brother shouted. I had to admit, he had guts. The kid could barely stand.

Luna continued to struggle. Releasing her with a curse, Gino turned and pointed his gun at Logan. "I *will* kill him!" he shouted.

Luna froze halfway to me, her head whipping around to her brother, then back to me. Her eyes pleaded with me for a second before she took a step back toward him. "Please," she told her father. "Please, Gino. Don't do it."

"Let them go," I told him again. "Let them go and I'll come with you without a fight."

"How do I know I can believe you?" he asked me.

"You can't," I replied. "But that's part of the appeal, isn't it?"

He studied me for a long time. I waited for the terror to overwhelm me, but I felt nothing at all as I waited for him to make up his mind. No fear. No disgust for what I offered. Instead, I wondered if there was any chance at all that Luna would forgive me if Gino turned down my offer. Because if that happened, I was fully prepared to rush him and wrestle that fucking gun out of his hand while she ran. And if her brother got shot in the process, well, it would be one less person for me to worry about.

"Deal," he sneered. A second later, four more of his men rushed into the warehouse. Under Gino's orders, three of them aimed their weapons at me while the fourth one zip tied my wrists behind my back so tight it cut off my circulation. I hissed at the touch of his fingers on my skin, but I allowed him to do it.

Luna shook her head as tears ran unnoticed down her cheeks. "Tristan, no. Don't do this."

I turned my attention to her brother. "My SUV is parked in the next lot." His one good eye left Gino and landed on me when he realized I was talking to him. "The keys are under the mat. Take your sister and get her the fuck out of here."

He turned back to Gino, who lowered his gun now that I was under control. "Go on," Gino told him. "A deal is a deal. And unlike your sister, I live up to my promises."

Without a word, Logan hobbled forward and tried to grab Luna with his good hand. She wrapped her arm around his waist, but she wouldn't leave. "We can't," she told him, her voice thick with tears. "Logan, we can't just leave him here."

"Yes," he told her. "We can." He tried to make her move, but he was too weak from his injuries.

"Luna."

Her dark blue eyes were luminous from her tears as they darted to mine. Her nose was running and her cheeks were blotchy.

And she was fucking stunning.

"I'll come for you," I told her. "I promise."

"Take them out of here," Gino told one of his men.

But Luna just dug in her heels. "No." She shook her head. "No. I'm not leaving you here with him."

I stepped closer to her, ignoring her brother and the shouts of Gino's men. They wouldn't shoot me. It would ruin all of Gino's fun. Catching her eyes with mine, I forced her to look at me. "You have to go," I said quietly. "Or he'll kill you. And I can't live with that."

"What about you?" she threw back at me. "What am I supposed to do knowing what's happening to you? What if he kills *you*?"

"Well, then you'll be free, *bambolina*."

Startled, she stared at me.

"Luni..."

Tearing her eyes away from me, she looked up at her brother, who was swiftly losing his fight to stay on his feet.

I stepped back. "Go," I ordered. "Get your brother out of here." I didn't know where Gino was going to take me, or if Luca and Enzo would find me in time, but I exhaled a deep breath of relief as she released a sob, accusing me with her eyes before she dropped them to the floor and they started making their way out of the warehouse.

She didn't look back.

I watched them until they were out of the building, and then I turned to face the only man who, deep down, I still feared.

He smiled, and a cold sweat broke out on my skin.

CHAPTER 5

Luna

My back and shoulders screamed in pain as I helped Logan to the store parking lot where Tristan had left his SUV. A few cars slowed down as they drove past, but no one stopped to help us. Not that I wanted them to. Unless it was a street gang packing weapons and a doctor in the car, they couldn't do anything for us.

Tears blurred my vision, and I tripped more than once, almost sending us both sprawling onto the pavement. It was only by sheer force of will that I kept us upright, because I knew if we fell, I'd never get Logan up again.

For the second time, I stopped and looked back over my shoulder, horrified at myself that I'd left Tristan there with the monster who was my father.

I stopped walking. I needed to go back...

"Luni..." Logan's weight on my spine nearly doubled as he swayed on his feet.

"We're almost there," I told him as I got us moving again, my heart ripping apart with every step. "We're almost there, honey. Just hold on." I didn't know the extent of his injuries, but he was fading fast. I needed to get him to the hospital.

With strength I didn't know I possessed, I managed to get us both to the car and dumped him into the passenger side. Then I ran around the front of the vehicle and ripped open the driver's side door, found the keys, and climbed in.

"We need...to call the...cops," Logan choked out beside me. His words were slow as he fought to stay conscious.

I pulled my cell out of the pocket of my jeans, but instead of dialing 911, I sat there staring at the black screen. "We can't," I told him. And that was when I realized I couldn't take him to a hospital, either. If I did, the police would be called. And what the hell was I supposed to tell them? That our capo father who we didn't even know was still alive kidnapped his son and beat the hell out of him only because he knew his daughter would come running to save him so he could rape her some more if she could get out of the cell the other mafia guy was keeping her in to keep her safe from said father?

They'd take one look at me and my background as a sex worker and blow us off at best. Or at worst, they'd start sticking their noses into mafia business and get themselves killed. And us, too.

"We can't call the cops."

I put my phone back in my pocket, my mind spinning as I sat there staring at the warehouse through my tears. Would the SUV still be drivable if I smashed it through the wall? Probably not. And I had Logan to think about. I needed to get medical help for him. But where the fuck was I supposed to go?

"Luni..."

Glancing over at my little brother, I watched his face contort in agony a second before his head fell forward onto his chest. He'd passed out, and a part of me was grateful. I reached over him and fastened the seatbelt across his body so he wouldn't fall forward if I had to brake fast. Then, with shaking hands, I wasted precious seconds trying to get the key into the ignition.

The SUV started easily, and I threw it into drive and almost drove us right into traffic. Stomping on the brake pedal, I skidded to a stop, my eyes going between the half-finished warehouse next door and my little brother's bloody and swollen face.

With a cry of anguish that rose from the very depths of me, I quickly checked for cars and hit the gas pedal.

Even unconscious, Logan's ragged breathing filled the car, and I sped through the city streets, weaving in and out of traffic with reckless abandon.

I headed in the general direction of Luca's lake house because I didn't know where else to go. I couldn't remember exactly how to get there, and wished I'd paid more attention when I'd left with Veda.

Veda!

Getting off the next exit, I pulled the SUV over to the side of the road and found the number she'd given me.

"Luna! Are you and your brother okay? Did Tristan find you? I'm sorry, but I called him. I was worried."

"Does Luca have access to a doctor?"

"Yes, of course."

Thank god. Except I didn't know how to get there. "How do I get back to his house?"

After a brief pause, she asked, "Isn't Tristan with you?"

My throat tightened, choking off my response, as the world outside blurred behind my tears.

"Luna?"

I shook my head, unable to answer.

"Luna? Where is he?"

"Gino." I forced the hated name out of my mouth. "Gino has him..." I trailed off.

"Oh shit."

"Veda! My brother needs a doctor!"

"Where are you now?"

I gave her my general location.

"Okay, you're close. Let me give you the address."

"Hang on." Putting her on speakerphone, I pulled up my maps app. "Okay."

She rattled off the address to Luca's house. "I'll call and let him know you're coming."

"Thank you," I whispered. "Thank you, Veda."

"Be careful. I'm coming home and I'll see you soon," she told me, and ended the call.

Ten minutes later, I pulled up to the gates. They were closed, two armed guards standing sentinel. But as soon as they saw me and Logan, they opened them and waved me through.

Parking the SUV, I left Logan in the car and ran up the couple of steps to the front door. It swung open right as I got to it and Enzo stepped back to let me in. I burst through the doorway, my voice shrill with panic. Luca entered the room from a hallway to the right. "Please! My brother needs help. He needs a doctor."

"Is he in the car?" Enzo asked.

I nodded, my throat constricting with emotion, rendering me unable to speak as I followed him back out of the house. The gravity of the situation crashed over me like a tidal wave now that we'd arrived at Luca's house. I couldn't stop shaking and my heart was racing. Tears pricked at the corners of my eyes as the overwhelming fear for my brother's life—and Tristan's—consumed me.

Luca followed us. "Where is Tristan?"

I didn't answer him as Enzo opened the passenger door and unhooked the seatbelt so he could get Logan out. I was afraid to.

Luca grabbed my arm hard enough to leave bruises and spun me around. "This is Tristan's SUV. Where the FUCK is he?"

I stared into his cold blue eyes. "He...he..."

"WHERE IS HE?" he roared.

"Gino!" I screamed back. "He traded himself for us. He's with Gino!"

Yanking me into his hard body, he sneered down into my face. "You allowed him to do that? And you left him there?"

"I had to!" I told him. "My brother needs help."

His voice was like ice when he said, "*Fuck* your brother."

I stared up at him and slammed my mouth shut. I had no argument. He was right. I shouldn't have left him there. There was no excuse. I should've at least tried. "My brother is all I have," I whispered. "Please. Help him."

"Luca, let her go."

After a moment, he did. Glancing over at Enzo as he pulled Logan out of the vehicle, he gave me one last glare and then went over to help him. "The doctor is on his way," he told me. "We're going to get your brother in the house, and then you're going to tell me *exactly* where you left Tristan. And god help you if he's not alive when we get there."

Lightheaded with relief, I nodded. "Thank you."

With another chilling look, he went to help Enzo get Logan into the house, yelling for someone named Lisa.

A middle-aged woman with warm eyes and a worried frown rushed into the cavernous room from the back of the house. "I've got the bed set up," she told Luca. "Veda called me. Bring him in."

We went through a pair of glass-paned French doors into what looked like a sitting room or office area. But instead of a desk, there was a hospital bed set up in the center of the room. A couple of light blue chairs with round glass end tables were near the floor-to-ceiling windows.

Once they had Logan on the bed, Luca turned back to me. "Where exactly did you leave him?"

I told him everything without pausing, even when tears ran down my face and my nose got all stuffy and my voice broke.

When I was finished, he nodded once, and with a glance at Enzo, they turned and left.

Part of me wanted to run after them, and I felt like I was being torn in two.

"Don't worry, they'll bring Tristan home."

I'd almost forgotten the woman—Lisa—was there. She handed me a tissue, and I used it to clean up my face while taking a few seconds to pull myself together. "Thank you," I told her.

She smiled and opened her mouth to say something, but the doorbell rang. "That'll be the doctor. I'll be right back."

The man that came back with her was younger than I thought he'd be, but he was completely professional as he shoved his short brown hair off his forehead and adjusted his wire-framed glasses. Setting down his bag, he started firing off questions as he carefully untied Logan's wrists.

I told him what I knew and tried to stay out of his way while Lisa helped him strip off Logan's clothes so he could better check his injuries.

"Will he be okay?" I asked him when I couldn't take the suspense anymore.

"He was beaten badly," he stated. "His arm is obviously broken. One of his cheekbones might be shattered. I'll need to take some X-rays of his torso." He glanced over at me. "And as soon as I'm done here, I'll take a look at your face."

I gingerly touched my cheek, wincing as my fingertips brushed against the swollen, tender skin. In the chaos of getting Logan the hell away from Gino, I'd completely forgotten about my own injuries. Adrenaline must've masked the pain, but now that things had settled down, I could feel the throbbing ache radiating from my cheek where I'd hit the floor and the soreness in my back from Gino's knee.

Lisa left and returned a few minutes later with a metal rolling cart. "What's that?" I asked her.

"A portable X-ray machine," she told me. "And this is a handheld sonogram. The doctor can hook it up to his phone and take scans of your brother's organs."

I collapsed in one of the blue chairs so I was out of the way and watched as the doctor took X-rays and scans of Logan's battered body. I couldn't lose my brother. He was all I had left in this world.

After what felt like hours, but was probably closer to thirty minutes, he set aside his instruments and turned to me. "He has a broken arm, three cracked ribs, and a lot of deep tissue bruising. His eye socket is fractured but not shattered. I didn't see any internal bleeding, but keep an eye out for any swelling in his abdomen or any other strange symptoms. I'll leave some pain meds here for him in case he needs them, and I'll brace up that arm until we can get a proper cast put on him. It's good that he's not awake for this."

I took a shaky breath. "So he's going to be okay?"

He nodded. "With rest and time, yes."

Tears of relief sprang to my eyes. "Thank you," I whispered.

"You're welcome. Now, let's get his arm taken care of and then I'll take a look at your face."

Lisa helped him with Logan's arm. He groaned in his sleep when the doctor set it, but didn't wake up. Then Lisa held it still while he went out to his car and got the brace for it.

Then he pulled up the other chair, and I let him examine me, wincing when he pressed along my cheekbone and jaw. "Nothing seems to be broken," he said after a moment. "And these cuts are superficial and shouldn't scar. You'll have a hell of a bruise, though. Wash your face with some soap and water to clean out this scraped section so you don't get an infection, and you should be fine. Is this your only injury?"

I frowned. "Um, I was hit with something. Across my right shoulder and head."

He didn't ask any questions as he probed those areas. "I think you're okay. How long ago did this happen?"

I shook my head. "I'm not sure. A couple of hours, maybe."

"Will you be with her until the guys get back?" he asked Lisa.

She nodded. "I can check on them both."

"If she falls asleep, wake her up every few hours and ask her some questions." He turned back to me. "You might have a concussion. If you start having headaches, blurred vision, dizziness, or anything out of the ordinary, have someone call me."

I nodded and stood. "Okay. Thank you," I said again as I stood up.

Lisa left with the doctor, leaving me alone with my unconscious brother. I pulled the blanket over his chest and then dragged one of the chairs over to his bedside and sank down into it. Taking his hand in both of mine, I watched his chest rise and fall. Silent tears slipped down my cheeks, but whether they were from relief that Logan was going to be okay or fear for Tristan, I couldn't say.

The rational part of my brain knew I'd done what I had to do, that I couldn't have gotten us all out of there intact. But the other part of me, the part that cared for Tristan more than I wanted to admit, was screaming at me for abandoning him.

Please be okay, I prayed to whoever would listen. *Please...*

The door opened behind me, and I twisted around, hoping my prayers had been answered, even though I knew it was impossible that they'd be back so soon.

But it was Veda. Still dressed in her skirt and blouse from earlier, she rushed over and dropped to her knees beside my chair, throwing her arms around me. "I'm so glad you're okay," she said, her voice thick with emotion.

I hugged her back, fresh tears burning my eyes. "I left him behind, Veda. I left Tristan with Gino. He traded himself for us and I just...I left him there."

"Gino?" Her mouth twisted in disgust. "I never liked that guy. Luca told me how you ended up as his date for the wedding."

"There's more to it than that." Tired of being strong, I poured my heart out to this woman who was little more than a stranger to me. I told her everything, starting with the poker game and ending with Tristan letting me out of the cell and getting the text from my brother. I even told her how Logan and I had grown up in foster care. I skipped over the more intimate moments between me and Tristan and the details of what I'd done to protect my brother. Not because I didn't want her to know, but because I didn't know if he could hear me.

When I was finished and sat there in a puddle of my tears, she got up and came back with the box of tissues, which she handed to me. "Gino won't be alive much longer. Will that upset you?"

I looked up at her, surprised. I'd expected sympathy. A hug. The usual girly bullshit. "What do you mean?"

"I mean, Luca's going to kill him. He told me the other night that's always been his plan. He's just had to wait for the right time."

CHAPTER 6

Tristan

Something clenched in my chest, a mixture of relief and dread washing over me as Luna and her brother made it outside without anyone stopping them. She was safe.

But at what cost?

I turned back to Gino. His eyes glinted with sadistic glee, reveling in my surrender. "Well, well, well," he sneered. "So there *is* a heart in there, after all."

I remained silent, steeling myself for the inevitable terrors that awaited me. Gino stepped closer, his breath hot against my face. "You know what this means, don't you, boy? You're mine now. Just like old times."

Old times. The words echoed in my mind, conjuring a flood of painful memories. The beatings, the rapes, the humiliation, the scars that marred my body and soul. I had escaped that hell once before, vowing never to return. Yet here I stood, willingly offering myself up to the devil himself.

For her.

For Luna.

The realization hit me like a punch to the gut. I'd just sacrificed everything—my body, my freedom, my sanity, possibly even my life—for a woman I barely knew if you really thought about it. A woman who had somehow managed to pierce through the impenetrable walls I had built around myself.

Jesus Christ. What the fuck was wrong with me?

She was beautiful, and fierce, and I couldn't get enough of her body. But was that all it took for me to sacrifice myself? Or was it the way she looked at me, as if she saw past the monster and glimpsed the broken man beneath?

I didn't have time to ponder the answers. Gino's men surrounded me, their guns trained on my every move. "Take him to the car," Gino commanded. "And don't trust him for a second. *È furbo, questo qui.*" He's smart, this one.

As they dragged me away, the weight of my decision settled heavily upon my shoulders, threatening to crush me under its burden.

But a flicker of something else burned within me. Something I had thought long dead.

Hope.

Hope that, somehow, I would find my way back to her. That I would survive whatever Gino had planned for me until either Luca and Enzo could find me or I could escape.

Until then, I would endure. For Luna, it seemed, I would endure anything.

The car ride was a blur of pain. Gino's men had taken his words to heart and decided to do what they could to incapacitate me before they threw me into the back seat of one of the cars. Every bump in the road sent a sharp jolt of agony to my aching head, where the butt of one of their pistols had smashed into my temple. For a few minutes, I drifted in and out of consciousness, my mind conjuring images of Luna to keep me sane.

Her smile. The little sounds of pleasure she made when I touched her. The way she looked at me with those piercing blue eyes, as if she could see into the darkest, ugliest depths of my soul.

I clung to those memories like a lifeline as Gino took me farther and farther away from her.

The car finally came to a stop, and two of Gino's men dragged me unceremoniously out of the back seat. I had no idea how long we'd been driving, but I'd been fully conscious for a while now. I blinked against the harsh glare of the sun, trying to get my bearings. We were at a large ranch house, surrounded by nothing but barren Texas desert as far as the eye could see. There were no trees, no hills. Just dirt and scrub brush. There was nowhere anyone could hide. And even if they could, the dust clouds it would kick up would give away any vehicles heading this way, if by some miracle the guys on top of the house didn't spot them first.

There was no way Luca and Enzo would be able to get anywhere near this place. They'd have to bring an army with them to even have a chance.

I was hauled across the dirt yard and thrown into a dank, musty outbuilding. The door slammed shut behind me, plunging me into darkness. I lay there on the hard concrete floor, shivering from the cold, my shoulders throbbing with pain from my hands being tied so tight behind my back as a fucking freight train ran through my head.

Now that I had a moment to myself, the weight of what I'd done truly began to hit me. Did I regret giving up my life for hers? Honestly, I couldn't say. In that moment, all I could think about was doing whatever I had to do to get Luna the fuck out of there.

In the short time I'd had with Luna, I'd felt something I never thought possible. I felt alive for the first time in my life. Really, truly alive. Like there was something in life to look forward to.

And it appeared I would endure a thousand lifetimes of pain and suffering just to feel that way again.

My peace was shattered when the door opened and a bulky figure filled the doorway. I blinked against the sunlight, but I knew who it was before he even opened his mouth.

Gino left the door open as he came inside, followed by two of his men. I wasn't surprised when they stayed near the doorway, watching but not participating. They were there to make sure I didn't get loose while Gino did... whatever the fuck he was going to do to me. Nothing more. Nothing less.

Pain exploded across my jaw as his fist connected with my jaw. The taste of blood, metallic and coppery, filled my mouth. He grabbed a fistful of my hair, wrenching my head back. "You always were a pain in my ass," he growled, his breath hot and fetid against my cheek. "Killing my men. Stealing my daughter!" His upper lip lifted into a sneer. "I knew you had her. You think you're above me now. But I'll break you again, boy. Just like I did before."

I spat a mouthful of blood into his face. "Fuck you," I rasped.

He laughed, a cruel, mirthless sound that sent chills down my spine as he wiped at his face with the sleeve of his jacket without letting go of my hair. "I'm glad you haven't lost your spirit," he told me. "It'll make this so much more fun."

Releasing me, he ambled over to a weathered wooden table I hadn't noticed when they'd thrown me in here. They'd closed the door, shutting off the light, before I'd had a chance to really look around. He picked something up off the table and turned to face me. The crackle of electricity filled the air, blue sparks dancing along two metal prongs. The acrid stench of ozone assaulted my nostrils.

I was well acquainted with the cattle prod in his hands. Narrowing my eyes, I cocked my head, waiting for the fear that would paralyze a normal man. But although I wasn't looking forward to being shocked, immobilizing terror never came. "You won't break me," I told him. "At least not before I kill you."

"We'll see about that, boy." He pressed the prod against my side and white-hot agony ripped through me. My body convulsed, muscles seizing and spasming as the current tore through me. I bit back a scream, determined not to give him the satisfaction. Pain, I could handle. Pain was home.

When it was over, I rolled to my side and sat up, breathing hard. Gino's eyes were bright with excitement, and a large bulge stretched out the front of his pants. This was what he lived for. I wondered how many other boys, or men, he'd tortured like this for no other reason except that it got him off. Causing pain was foreplay to someone as sick as Gino.

He shocked me again and again, until my body went slack from the pain. When he didn't get the reaction from me he hoped for, he decided he was bored and threw the cattle prod back onto the table. Every muscle in my body was sore and my nerve endings were on fire. My mouth hung open as I sucked in air and spit ran down my chin. Turning my head, I wiped my beard on my shoulder.

I wasn't so foolish to think he was done with me. But when my eyes caught his, I smiled, imagining the way he would scream like a woman when I carved open his stomach, reached through his guts, and pulled out his balls.

Gino drew back for a moment before his expression hardened. Stalking toward me, he grabbed the collar of my shirt. I reacted violently to the touch of his fingers on my bare skin, jerking backward so hard the material ripped.

No. No. NO!

I could take pain. I could take torture. But his hands on my body...his dick in my ass...his fat body fucking me in front of his men as they laughed and spit in my face...

The memories of my past burst into my conscience and I was suddenly a child once again. My entire body began to tremble violently. I couldn't stop it. I couldn't stop *him*. I was too small. Too weak.

Just as the screams I'd suppressed welled up in my throat, the sound of gunfire shattered the air. Shouts and screams followed, along with the unmistakable staccato of semi-automatic weapons.

Releasing my shirt, Gino whirled around, his eyes widening in shock and rage. "What the hell is going on out there?" he roared. "Go! Go!" he shouted to the guards at the door. He pulled his gun from inside his jacket and ran out of the building, leaving me sagging against my bonds.

Closing my eyes, I swallowed hard.

More gunfire, closer this time. Fighting the demons in my head who at last had decided to come out and play, I struggled to get to my feet, but kept falling over.

Tires crunched on gravel outside and dust floated through the open doorway. A flicker of hope sparked in my chest when I heard my name. Luca and Enzo. It had to be.

Perhaps I'd underestimated my friends.

After a few anxious seconds, Luca charged in, his gun drawn. Relief crashed over me at the sight of him and my breath hitched as something caught in my chest.

"Tristan!" Luca's eyes widened in horror as he took in my battered state. "Jesus Christ. Are you all right?"

I nodded, unable to find the words to speak.

He holstered his gun and drew a wicked-looking knife, slicing through my bonds with quick, efficient strokes. I collapsed forward and he caught me, lowering me gently to the floor as my shoulders screamed in agony.

"I got you, T," he murmured. "I got you. Let's get you the fuck out of here."

I tried once again to stand, but my knees buckled beneath me. Luca caught me before I hit the ground, his strong arms wrapping around my waist. A violent sound was wrenched from my throat and my body tried to jerk away, but he held me fast. "I'm sorry," he murmured, his voice low and soothing. "I'm sorry, but I've got to get you out of here."

He half-carried, half-dragged me from the building and into the waning sunlight. I squinted against the glare, my eyes watering from the sudden brightness. The scene that greeted me was one of utter chaos.

Bodies littered the ground, their blood staining the dusty earth a deep crimson. Enzo was behind the SUV, covering our escape. Blood stained his white shirt and black jacket, as it did Luca's, but neither of them appeared injured. Bullets hit the vehicle and the dirt all around him, and he returned fire whenever he could.

He turned as we approached, his eyes widening at the sight of me. "*Cazzo*," he swore. "What the hell did that *bastardo* do to you?"

I shook my head to let him know my injuries weren't as bad as he thought. "Gino," I rasped, my voice hoarse and raw. "Where is he?"

Enzo's jaw clenched. "I don't know. I haven't seen him."

Rage surged through me, white-hot and all-consuming. I pushed away from Luca, staggering a few steps before finding my balance. "I'm going after him," I growled. "I need to kill him."

Ignoring the bullets flying around us, Luca stepped in front of me, appearing so suddenly I almost fell on my ass. "We will, T. I promise you that. But right now, we need to get the fuck out of here and go somewhere safe. You're in no condition to go after him like this. And we can't hold these guys off much longer. There's too many of them and we're running out of bullets."

I stiffened. The training that was so ingrained in me rising to the surface. *I* should be protecting *him*, not the other way around. I wanted to argue, but I knew he was right. I could barely stand up straight. Reluctantly, I nodded in agreement and got into the SUV.

"Luca! Get in!"

Enzo opened the passenger side door and climbed over to the driver's side, with Luca right behind him. The SUV was built to withstand this kind of thing, but now that we were safe inside, we needed to get the fuck out of there before someone out there with half a brain decided to take out the tires.

As we sped away from the ranch, leaving the carnage behind us, I leaned my head back against the seat and closed my eyes, trying not to think about what would've happened if they hadn't shown up.

Suddenly, I jerked my head up. "Luna?"

"She's at the house with her brother," Luca told me.

Enzo glanced into the rearview mirror. "We're being followed."

"Just stay ahead of them," Luca said. "We'll lose them once we get back to the highway."

I tried to slow my racing heart. Every inch of my body ached, the aftershocks of the cattle prod still crackling through my muscles. But the physical pain was nothing compared to the rage that consumed me.

Gino had fucking escaped.

Again.

The man who had tortured me, broken me, turned me into the monster I was today, was still out there. And I now saw that as long as he drew breath, I would never be safe. *Luna* would never be safe. He'd gone rogue. Luca's position in the family wouldn't protect me anymore.

I clenched my fists, ignoring the sharp bite of my nails digging into my palms. I had to find him. I had to end this, once and for all.

But first, I needed to see *her*.

The tires squealed as Enzo took a sharp turn, throwing me against the door. I gritted my teeth against the fresh wave of pain that shot through me.

"Almost there," Luca said from the front seat, his voice tight with tension.

I didn't respond, my mind already racing ahead to the moment I would lay eyes on Luna again.

Once we made it to the highway, Enzo was able to lose the car following us before we hit rush hour traffic driving into Austin.

A hundred years later, the SUV finally rolled to a stop, and I was out the door before Enzo had even put it in park. I staggered, my legs nearly giving out beneath me, but I pushed forward, propelled by the desperate need to see her.

I burst through the front door, my heart hammering in my chest as Luca and Enzo yelled at me to wait.

And then she was there, her face a little battered but still beautiful, and I could breathe again.

CHAPTER 7

Luna

Veda's question rang in my ears.

Gino won't be alive much longer. Will that upset you?

I thought about everything that fucker had done and shook my head. "I can't believe I'm saying this," I told her. "But no. I don't think that will bother me at all." Wiping my face with a tissue, I blew my nose. "He's my father by blood, but that's it. He's never done anything for me but donate his sperm. And right now, he's doing god only knows what to Tristan." My voice broke and fresh tears filled my eyes.

"Tristan told you to leave," she said as she pulled up the other chair.

Pulling myself together, I looked her straight in the eyes. "Would you have left Luca?"

She didn't so much as blink. "Yes. If he ordered me to."

"You're lying," I told her, trying to smile, but my face wouldn't cooperate.

She gave me a little shrug. "Maybe. I've never been in that situation, thank god, so I've never had to test it."

"And Luca, as far as I know, has never gone through the shit Tristan has with Gino." The words caught in my throat as guilt threatened to consume me. I hadn't told her the sordid details of Tristan's traumatic past with my father. Those dark secrets weren't mine to share, and I would never betray his trust like that.

She gave me an encouraging smile, and then said, "Tristan scares the ever-living fuck out of me, Luna. I'm sure he'll hold his own until Luca and Enzo can get there."

But she didn't know. She didn't know what Gino had done to him when he was a child, or the effect those memories still had on him. But all I said was, "I hope so."

We sat in silence after that. Lisa brought me a cup of coffee and a sandwich, but I couldn't eat. I just held Logan's hand, careful not to jar his broken arm. Veda was with me the entire time, kicking off her shoes and curling her legs underneath her. I appreciated the company even if I didn't feel like talking.

The sun had dropped beneath the horizon when I heard the front door open and close, followed by raised voices. My heart leaped into my throat, and I jumped to my feet, running out of the room with Veda close on my heels.

Luca and Enzo were back, and they had Tristan with them. He was alive and had blood smeared across the side of his neck, but he was walking on his own. Sort of. He was a bit unsteady. As he got closer, I saw his long-sleeved shirt was ripped at the neckline, revealing a peek at some of his scars, but otherwise, he seemed intact.

"Oh my god," I whispered, my hand flying to my mouth. "Tristan..."

His eyes shot over to me, and he froze. "Luna." His voice was strong, and although his face showed nothing of what he was feeling, I thought I heard a hint of relief.

Tears spilled down my cheeks as I rushed forward, wanting to throw my arms around him, but not sure how he would react. He seemed distant again. Guarded. I stopped when I got close enough that he could touch me if he wanted to. "I'm so sorry," I sobbed. "I'm so sorry I left you there. I had to help Logan, and you told me to go and...and I didn't know what else to do."

"Shh," he soothed, reaching out to cup my injured cheek with a gentle hand. "You did the right thing, *bambolina*. If you'd stayed, we'd both be dead right now."

A pained sound tore from my throat at the endearment, and I leaned into his touch, my tears wetting his palm.

My cheek stung where his palm touched the raw spots, but I didn't care. "I thought...I was so scared. I didn't know if Luca and Enzo would get there on time. I thought...I thought he killed you," I finally forced out.

"Not yet," he said, so quietly I almost didn't hear him as he brushed his thumb along the tender skin beneath my eye, then he dropped his hand.

I wanted to ask him if anything else had happened. If Gino had...hurt him in any other way. But I wouldn't ask him such a thing with everything there, and the fact that he hadn't locked himself in his cell gave me hope. So, instead, I asked, "Did you kill him?"

He shook his head. "No."

"But..." I looked to Luca and Enzo, noticing for the first time that they weren't in much better shape. "I don't understand. How is he still alive if you're here?" I'd assumed they would take Gino out the first chance they could. I'd *hoped* they would. After what he'd done to the both of us—and to Logan—it was no less than he deserved.

"He must've run off when we arrived," Enzo told me as Luca pressed a kiss to the top of Veda's head. She stood in the circle of his arms, completely uncaring if the blood on him was getting on her clothes, and I was almost envious of how sure she was of her welcome there.

"They'd left the construction site," he continued. "But we were able to track T's phone. By the time we caught up to them, Gino had more men with him, and it turned into a goddamn bloodbath."

Tristan's expression was unreadable as he stared down at me. He'd never taken his eyes from me since he'd walked in.

My heart lurched. This man had faced down his worst nightmare to save me and Logan. Well, to save me, at least. I didn't really think he cared at all about people in general besides Luca and Enzo.

And now me.

As Veda talked to Luca and Enzo, I swallowed hard, wondering again what it was about me that caught and held his attention that first day he saw me. And at the same time, feeling sick at the thought of him caught in the middle of this shit between me and Gino because I'd been stupid enough to believe Gino would ever let me go.

"You're wrong," he told me quietly.

My eyes jerked to his as he read my thoughts. "I am?"

"He didn't want you. He wanted me. He knew I'd come after you, and he knew I'd come alone."

I crossed my arms over my chest and hugged myself. *What does that mean?* I wanted to scream.

Tristan turned as though to leave, and I reached out to stop him. He flinched at my touch, and I pulled my hand back like I'd been burned as my heart cracked into jagged pieces. "I just... Are you hurt?"

He studied me for a long moment. "I'm fine," he told me dismissively. "I need to get cleaned up."

But he wasn't fine. I could see it in the tightness around his eyes and hear it in the emotionless tone of his voice.

I watched him walk away toward the back of the house, his back stiff and straight, and I forced myself to let him go, even though a part of me wanted to go after him, to demand he talk to me, or at the very least let me hold him. But I knew it would be useless. I couldn't reach him right now.

"Luna," Veda said softly from behind me. "Why don't you try to get some rest? Logan's probably out for the night, and I'm sure Luca will let you use one of the spare rooms. It's been a long day."

I shook my head, wiping at my tears. "I'm not leaving my brother. He'll be scared if he wakes up and doesn't know where he is."

Veda sighed. "Are you sure? You look exhausted. I can sit with him."

"Thanks, but no. I need to be there. I'll rest later," I promised her when she looked like she was going to argue more. I couldn't leave Logan right now, despite the weariness seeping into my bones. With one last longing look in the direction Tristan had gone, I left them all standing in the great room and returned to Logan's room with determined steps. Sinking into the chair beside him, I resumed my vigil at his bedside as I tried not to read too much into Tristan's reactions to me, or mine to him.

Pulling the photo of me and my mother from my back pocket, a shadow of doubt slid down my spine. Maybe it was better this way. I hadn't forgotten about this picture, or what it could mean. If anything, it only made my feelings for my captor—my savior—even more complicated.

I shouldn't care about him. But how could I not after everything he'd done for me? He'd risked his life—more than once—to keep me safe from Gino. Even if I didn't agree with his methods, was I just supposed to ignore that?

And the worst thought of all—the one that made my breath catch and new tears fill my eyes—what if after today he realized I wasn't worth it after all?

The minutes ticked by slowly as I waited for the night to pass and the next day to dawn. Everything always looked better by the light of day. Lisa brought me more coffee, along with a glass of water, but I left them both untouched on the end table. I couldn't stomach anything right now. Not until I knew Logan would be okay.

Veda came in a little while later wearing a clean white T-shirt and yoga pants. She was taking some college courses, she told me, and brought her homework in with her, asking if that was okay. I nodded and asked her about her classes, but, eventually, she left to get some sleep herself.

I must've dozed off at some point, though, because the next thing I knew, I felt Logan's hand twitch in mine. My eyes flew open, and I sat up straight, my heart pounding right out of my chest. The house was dark, but someone had turned on a lamp in the corner. It let off a muted glow, giving me enough light to make out his still features. "Logan?" I whispered.

His eyelids fluttered, then his good eye slowly opened and his hand slid up to hover over his ribs. He blinked a few times, frowning in confusion as he took in the tray ceiling and crown molding. Turning his head slowly, his gaze slid to the large windows, where lights flickered like fireflies on the other side of the dark lake, before coming back to land on me. "Luni? What..." He cleared his throat and lifted his head, looking around. "What happened? Where are we?"

Relief crashed over me, and I fought back tears. I was so fucking tired of crying. "You're okay," I said, squeezing his hand. "You've got a broken arm and some cracked ribs. Lots of bruising. But you're safe now."

He tried to sit up and winced, falling back against the pillows with a groan. "Where are we?" he asked again.

"Luca's house," I told him. "And be careful with your arm. It's just in a brace because the doctor didn't have anything to make the cast."

He glanced down at his arm. "Who the hell is Luca?"

"He's a..." I wasn't sure what to say. Criminal? Mob boss? Murderer? "...a friend."

"A friend, huh?"

I could tell he didn't believe me. And I didn't have a better explanation, so I just shrugged. "I'm sorry he hurt you," I told him when silence fell between us again. I didn't have to tell him that I was talking about Gino now.

Logan turned to me, his eyes filled with confusion and betrayal. "Is it true? Is Gino our father? Was everything he said true? About him? About *you?*"

I hesitated. I didn't want to lie to him, but I also didn't want to tell him the whole truth. Not yet. "It's...complicated," I said finally. "Would you like some water?"

"Uncomplicate it," he demanded, sounding more like himself despite the hoarseness of his voice. "How long have you known our father is alive?"

Standing, I strode over to the table where Lisa had brought in a cup and a straw along with a pitcher of water and poured some for him anyway. "Not that long."

"Why didn't you tell me?" He shook his head when I offered him a drink.

"I didn't know who he was until Tristan found out and took me from Gino's." I skipped the part about the cell.

"Wait. Who's Tristan?"

Another hard question to answer. "He's the guy who came after us."

"Your new boyfriend."

"I don't know," I told him honestly. "Maybe. Things are kind of a mess right now."

"He took you from our...from Gino?"

I nodded. "I met Tristan when Gino brought me here for a wedding. He thought I looked familiar. Eventually, he figured out who I was, and realized what Gino was doing, and that I didn't know I was his daughter, so he rescued me from our father and brought me here, where I'd be safe from him." It was a simplified version, but I wasn't ready to get into the details. Not yet.

Logan was quiet for a long time as he stared up at the ceiling.

I leaned over him, searching his swollen face anxiously. "Are you okay? The doctor left you some pain meds if you need them."

"I'm fine. I don't want them."

"Logan, you're safe here. We both are. You don't have to worry about anything."

He looked at me then. "Luni, our father is some kind of gangster, isn't he?" He didn't wait for me to respond. "And have you looked at the guy who came after you? Like, really looked at him? That's one scary motherfucker."

"I know," I told him. "He's a bit...closed off. And protective. But he won't let anything happen to us." I fussed with his blanket. I'd see if someone could get him some more comfortable clothes tomorrow. He was still in his jeans and T-shirt, although I'd taken off his sneakers earlier. "You need to sleep."

"Why would he want him instead of us?"

I thought about how to explain. "They have a history."

He looked at me, then looked away. "Do you have a mirror?" he asked me suddenly.

"Uh..." I glanced around the room. "No."

"Would you bring me one? I want to see what that son of a bitch did to my pretty face."

I laughed. "I'm not sure that you do, honey."

He started to grin and then winced.

"Get some sleep, Logan. I'll stay right here with you. I promise."

I thought he was going to argue with me, but then he took as deep a breath as he could manage and his eye started drifting shut. "I'm not done with my questions, Luni."

"I know."

"You're gonna answer them." His words were barely more than a mumble, but I understood him well enough.

"I know," I whispered. "I will."

I stayed by Logan's side until he fell asleep. When I was sure he wouldn't wake up again, I slipped out of the room.

The house was dark and quiet, but I couldn't even think about trying to sleep myself. My mind was too full of everything that had happened over the last twenty-four hours.

Had it really only been a day? It felt like a lifetime.

With the soft lights underneath the cabinets leading me to it, I made my way to the kitchen on the other side of the house, thinking I'd rummage around and see if I could find any decaf tea.

I froze when I saw Tristan standing at the island. His back was to me, his hands braced on the edge of the counter, and his head bowed. From the doorway, I could smell the dark forest scent of him that told me he'd showered, and he'd changed into a long-sleeved, black cotton shirt and black sweatpants. His dark hair was still damp and brushed back from his face.

I didn't move, not wanting to startle him. He looked so vulnerable standing there, his shoulders slumped, his head down. Like he was carrying the weight of the world on his shoulders.

And maybe he was.

All the things he'd done to protect me flashed through my mind as I watched him. How he'd risked his life to save me from Gino. How he'd brought me to his home—to his cell—to keep me safe. The only place he ever really felt that way. How he'd helped me save Logan, even though I knew it was only me he'd wanted.

But then I thought about the picture in my pocket. The one of me and my mother. The one that I'd found in his safe.

God, I didn't know what to think. I didn't know how to feel. Everything was so mixed up inside me, and I wished I'd never gone snooping around his fucking house. But I had. And there was no going back now.

And I was NOT going back into that fucking cell.

I must have made a noise, because Tristan's head snapped up and he turned around, his dark eyes finding mine across the room. For a moment, we just stared at each other, the air between us charged with everything we weren't saying.

Then he straightened, his expression shuttering, and I knew the moment was over.

Feeling around on the wall, I found the light switch and flicked one of them on. More lights came on behind him.

"I thought you'd be sleeping," he said, his voice low and rough.

I shook my head. "I was just looking for some tea."

He studied me for a long moment. "Have you eaten? Are you hungry?"

"No, I'm not hungry."

Moving to the cabinets, he pulled out a box of herbal tea and showed it to me.

"That'll be perfect," I told him, my voice barely above a whisper.

As he busied himself with the kettle, I glanced back toward Logan's room before I sank down onto one of the stools at the island, my legs suddenly feeling weak. Warily, I watched him. He was so at ease in the kitchen, his movements precise and efficient, and I wondered what he was thinking.

Did he regret saving me? Did he wish he'd never met me? Never gotten involved in my life? Or did he feel the same pull between us that I did? The same inexplicable connection that seemed to defy all logic and reason?

I didn't know. I didn't know anything anymore.

Except that, no matter what he'd done, no matter what secrets he was keeping…if I stayed here with Logan much longer, I didn't know if I'd be able to stay away from him.

And that terrified me more than anything else.

Because if he really was involved with the murder of my mother somehow, what did that say about me?

What kind of person was I, to be drawn to someone like that?

To feel things for him that I'd never felt for anyone else?

I stared down at my hands, my vision blurring with unshed tears. I felt so lost, so confused. I didn't know what to do. I didn't know how to reconcile the man who'd saved me with the man who might have destroyed my life.

But one thing I did know?

For my sake, and Logan's, I had to let him go.

Even if it destroyed me in the end.

CHAPTER 8

Tristan

As I stood in the kitchen, my heart pounding hard in my chest, I couldn't take my eyes from Luna. Even with one side of her face scraped and swollen and the delicate skin beneath her eyes shadowed from worry and lack of sleep, she was utterly beautiful to me.

What disturbed me, however, was my recent revelation of the price I would pay to keep that beauty in my life.

I'd thrown myself to the wolves without a thought of what that would do to the other people in my life. I wasn't here to give in to dramatic whims over a woman. I was here to protect my boss. And Luca's life was so much more significant than mine. He was the head of the entire family. Me? I was nothing.

Yes, he had Enzo. And Enzo was a dangerous man. But he had a wife now. A family. Unlike me, he hadn't been created for one purpose and one purpose only—to keep the boss of *la Cosa Nostra* alive.

Tearing my gaze away, I put on the teakettle and found some herbal tea in the cabinet. Is this what happened when a man allowed his cock to dictate his choices?

The appendage in question stirred in answer, despite the lingering soreness in my muscles.

The hours I'd spent with Gino today had fucked with me in all kinds of ways. The biggest one being that I'd turned myself over to that *bastardo* willingly, without a second thought—for her. Knowing what he would do to me and praying he would fucking kill me before I lost my mind completely, I'd traded my body for theirs. I was willing to not just give my life, but my sanity, for *her*.

Because of this sick obsession I had with her.

Luca and Enzo, the only two people in the world who'd ever meant anything to me, were nearly killed today because I'd risked everything...for *her*. I'd risked their lives, and my own...for *her*. Apparently, I would willingly walk into my own nightmares...

For. *Her*.

And yet, I was still here at Luca's home, unable to make myself leave because of this overwhelming need I had to protect her.

Over the last few hours, I'd wondered more than once who I would save if I had to make a choice: Luca? The man whose life my entire existence revolved around? Enzo? The next closest thing I'd ever had to a friend?

Or Luna? The woman who'd saved me from my demons and whose touch made me want to weep because of how much I craved it, even as it made me want to peel my own skin off.

I'm touching you. It's me you feel. These are my hands. My touch. You don't belong to him. I don't belong to him, either. Look at me! Look!

Seeing her in front of me now, I was beginning to think I knew the answer to that question.

The air squeezed from my lungs. I didn't know who I was anymore. Bits and pieces from yesterday flew round and round in the darkest corners of my mind. Luna's terrified blue eyes. Gino's sick taunts. Gunshots and Luca shouting my name.

Miraculously, we'd all survived, but so had Gino.

Yet, strangely enough, instead of running home and locking myself away until the demons in my head were choked and silenced, I'd found myself here at Luca's, looking for *her*.

And when she'd run out of that room, her dark blue eyes full of worry for me, I'd forgotten for a moment that she might know what a monster I truly was.

And, perhaps, so had she.

I'd walked away before she could remember. Before I saw the relief in her eyes turn to hatred. But I wasn't able to go far. Instead of going home, I'd hung around Luca's lake house, showering in the gym where I kept a change of clothes before Enzo and I met him in his office to discuss what had gone down with Gino.

And when we were finished, I'd offered to stay and watch the house so Enzo could go home to his new wife and I could stay near *her*. Disgust rolled through me. Followed almost immediately by the overpowering need to once again feel her hands on my skin and her body moving beneath me.

At first, I'd kept to the office, watching the security cameras. And when that wasn't enough, I took to prowling around the darkened house like a ghost, keeping to the shadows so she wouldn't notice me if she happened to look outside the makeshift hospital room where she held her vigil.

I'd watched her as she sat beside her brother, her hand resting on his arm as he slept, and something ugly had twisted inside of me. Was this what jealousy felt like, I wondered?

In the soft light of the lamp I'd turned on for her when she'd dozed off, her skin appeared paler than usual, almost luminescent. The dark waves of her hair, black as ink across the white sheets of the bed where she'd laid her head. She looked so peaceful, her long lashes fanning out against her cheeks, her full lips slightly parted as she breathed evenly in slumber.

Just like now, I'd stood there watching her for a long time, unable to tear my gaze away. Even in sleep, Luna captivated me, and I was powerless to resist her allure.

As always, my body craved to be next to her, to be inside of her. And a part of me had wanted to lift her into my arms and take her to a dark corner of the house where I could fuck her until she didn't even remember she had a brother. Until there was no one for her but me.

But I didn't. Partly because, if I were honest with myself, I was afraid. How would she look at me now that she'd found the photo, once her fear for me subsided and the reality of what I'd done came crashing down around us? Would those captivating cobalt eyes shine with hatred and disgust when they met mine? Would she be able to look at me at all? To see past the monster who'd ripped her away from the only parent who'd cared about her?

By murdering Luna's mother, I'd unknowingly crossed a line that couldn't be uncrossed. Yet the mere thought of existing without her now filled me with a suffocating dread I'd never experienced before. She'd become my obsession, my reason for breathing, and I feared that losing her would be the end of me.

But I feared that keeping her would be the end of us both.

The teakettle whistled and my hand trembled as I poured the steaming water into the cup, leaving the tea bag inside to steep before bringing it to her.

She wouldn't look at me. "Thank you."

I watched her blow on her tea as I waited for her to ask why I had the photo, trying to imagine what it would feel like to have those full, wet lips on my skin.

But she didn't ask. "Logan has a broken arm, some cracked ribs, and some deep bruising," she told me.

I didn't give a fuck about her brother's injuries. "He's young and healthy. He'll heal quickly."

She must've heard the disregard in my voice, for she looked at me then. "He's the only thing I have," she said quietly.

My skin grew hot and my stomach clenched. The only thing she had? What the fuck was I? Nothing? Did I mean nothing to her at all? Everything I'd done these last few weeks had been for *her*.

"Why are you looking at me like that?"

I didn't respond. I couldn't. It took every ounce of willpower I had to stay where I was when what I really wanted to do was wrap my hand around her lying throat.

She looked down at her tea, and when she raised her chin again, there were tears in her eyes. "I shouldn't have left you there with him." Her eyes searched mine as she waited for me to respond, to tell her she did the right thing. When I said nothing, she continued, "I should've left Logan in the car and came back for you."

I didn't try to console her. I'd told her to leave and she had. Had she known there was a bag of weapons in the back? I hadn't told them. My focus had been on her getting to safety.

But she was right, a part of me was...I tried to figure out what this fire was in my blood...*enraged*. With her, and perhaps more with myself. I wanted to see her tears. Her guilt. Wanted her to plead for my forgiveness.

"I'm really so sorry, Tristan." Her chin trembled and the corners of her mouth turned down as she fought back more tears. "I was so scared. And—"

"You think I wasn't scared?" I asked. It was more out of curiosity than anything. Ever since I'd first seen her, she'd dragged emotions from me I hadn't even known existed. Did she not see that?

"Oh, god." Covering her face with her hands, she began to sob quietly.

I frowned. I didn't like seeing her like this. "Luna."

She sniffed and wiped at her face as she raised her head. "What can I do?" she asked. "Please, just tell me what to do."

My eyes roamed over her face, wet with tears, her blue eyes luminescent in the soft lighting, then dropped to her breasts. It was strange, this anger I felt. I wanted to comfort her and punish her at the same time. "Get on your knees."

She stilled.

"Get on your knees," I repeated. "I want to feel your mouth on me."

After a moment, she set down her cup, rose from the stool, and came to stand in front of me on the other side of the island. Her eyes rose to mine, and I cocked my head, waiting to see what she would do.

Slowly, she lowered herself to her knees, her eyes on my groin before she ran them up my body to my face.

My lips parted and my cock swelled to the point of pain as I stared down at her. I wanted to feel her mouth wrapped around me so fucking bad that I was about to cum in my pants.

Silently, she stared up at me, waiting for me to tell her what to do next. But she wasn't with me. She was playing the whore. In her head, she was somewhere else. Despite the needs of my body, this wasn't what I wanted from her.

I took a step back. "Go back to your brother."

She frowned. "What?"

Walking around her, I left the kitchen and headed back to Luca's office. I put my hand over my heart, trying to slow its rapid beats, but my pulse pounded in my ears and waves of hot and cold washed over me until I was drenched with sweat.

When I reached the office, I closed the door behind me and sank down onto the couch. Pressing the heels of my hands into my eyes, I tried to make sense of the chaos raging inside me. For as long as I could remember, I'd been numb. Empty. A void where a soul should be. But now, with Luna, everything was different.

Emotions I couldn't even name clawed at my insides, tearing me apart. It was as if a dam had burst within me, unleashing a torrent of feelings I was wholly unprepared for. Anger, fear, jealousy, desire—they all swirled together in a maelstrom that threatened to consume me.

I wanted her with an intensity that bordered on madness. The mere thought of her sent my heart racing and my blood burning through my veins. But it wasn't just lust. No, it was something deeper. Something far more dangerous.

When I was with her, I felt alive for the first time in my non-existence. She made me want things I had no right to want. Made me feel things I didn't even know I was capable of feeling.

And yet, I couldn't stay away. Even now, with the memory of her tear-stained face still fresh in my mind, I craved her presence like a junkie craving his next fix. It was a sickness, this need I had for her. A weakness that would be my undoing.

I lifted my head, staring blankly at the wall across from me. How had it come to this? How had one woman managed to break through the walls I'd built so carefully around myself?

My first instinct was to reach for my knife and release these emotions battling inside of me, but Gino had taken it when I'd handed over my weapons.

So instead, I sat there on Luca's couch until I was able to get up and do my job. I didn't go to Luna again, and if she saw me wandering around the house in the darkness, she didn't acknowledge me.

The sun was rising when I heard footsteps on the stairs and looked up from the kitchen table to see Luca and Veda coming down. As always, Veda smiled nervously in greeting as she passed by me on her way to the fridge. Luca looked tired, but he gave me a small nod of acknowledgment as he entered the kitchen behind her and made a pot of coffee.

"You should go home and get some rest," he said, after he'd given Veda her cup and she went to go check on Luna and Logan. "I'm sure you've had a long night."

I glanced toward Luna when I heard her voice, the sweet tones flowing over me and warming me from the inside out. "Yes," I told him.

"Luna is welcome to stay here with her brother as long as she'd like. Veda is telling her now."

I nodded. I was sure she would want to stay close to him.

"You're not going to argue with me about that?"

Dragging my eyes away, I met his curious stare. "No."

He waited for me to say more, but I couldn't explain something to him I didn't understand myself. Pushing back my chair, I stood and asked, "What time do you need me back here?"

If he was surprised, he didn't push it. "I'll call you as soon as I find out what time everyone else will arrive."

Luca was gathering the family together to determine Gino's fate. Something that should've been done weeks ago, but I wasn't the boss. I didn't make those decisions. "I'll keep my phone near me."

As I walked toward the front door, he trailed behind me. "Aren't you going to let Luna know you're leaving?"

I didn't stop or glance her way. "No." Then I opened the door and stepped out into the crisp morning air.

CHAPTER 9

Luna

I stood by Logan's bedside, helping him sit up against the pillows so he could eat the lunch Lisa had brought in. The swelling around his eye was going down, his skin was turning interesting colors of green and blue, and he was still in a lot of pain from his ribs. But he was wide awake for the first time since yesterday, and I considered that a win.

I'd been with him all night and all morning, except for a short time when Veda offered me the use of a shower and a spare toothbrush along with some clean clothes, which I'd graciously accepted.

A knock sounded on one of the French doors and Luca stepped in. "I'm sorry to interrupt. How are you feeling, Logan?"

"This is Luca," I told him. "The owner of this house."

Logan gave him a once-over, his eyes lingering on the cut of Luca's expensive suit jacket and the holster strap visible beneath it. "I'll live. Thanks for letting us stay here."

"Of course," Luca said. "As Veda told you earlier, you're welcome to stay as long as you need. The doctor will be coming back to check on you tomorrow to see how you're healing up. And if there's anything else I can do, please don't hesitate to ask."

"Thanks," Logan repeated.

Luca turned to me. "Luna, the family is gathering for a meeting in about an hour. I was hoping you might come speak to them."

"Me? Why?"

"There are things they need to know, and it would be better if those things came directly from you."

It didn't take a rocket scientist to figure out what he was talking about. "You want me to tell them about Gino."

"Yes."

I hesitated, glancing at Logan. I hated to leave his side right now. He wasn't comfortable here, and his injuries likely made him feel even more vulnerable.

"It won't take long," Luca assured me. "As you lived with him for a time, you've had experiences with him no one else has. You don't have to go into any uncomfortable details. Just emphasize how unstable he is."

If I knew anything about Italian men, or men in general, it was that they paid women very little attention unless that woman was naked. "Can't you just tell them?"

The corners of his mouth lifted in a cold smile. "It'll have more of an impact coming from you directly," he said. When I didn't respond right away, he continued, "We have a much better chance of finding him if the entire family puts their manpower behind it. I just need to convince them to do that, and you can help me with that."

I didn't know why I was arguing with him. I knew damn well it was only for show that he was giving me a choice at all. "All right," I agreed reluctantly. "Yeah, I can do that."

"Thank you." He paused, glancing at Logan before taking me gently by the elbow and guiding me over to the windows. The sun was out, glittering off the water, and the sky was big and blue without a cloud to break up the wide expanse. It was beautiful.

Luca cleared his throat to get my attention. "I've wanted to take Gino out for a long, *long* time for what he did to Tristan. Unfortunately, I needed to secure my position in the family and collect more evidence before I could make a move without endangering any of our lives. My father's cronies never gave a shit about the history between them." The venom in his voice made chills run up and down my arms. "They knew what Gino did, and they didn't care. To them, Tristan wasn't a boy or a man, he was a machine. But to me, he's always been my friend. So I needed something else. Something that was a threat to the entire family and not just one boy whose life no one cared about. If you can prove Gino's not mentally stable, along with my proof that he's working with the Russians, we might have a chance. Do you understand?"

I nodded. I did understand. And I could see now that Luca wasn't uncaring. If he'd gone after Gino for what was considered a personal infraction, it would've come back on him, and he would've ended up in the ground right beside his father. Perhaps Tristan and Enzo, too. "I do," I told him. "But why are you telling me this?"

"I just wanted to emphasize how important this is." He paused, catching my eyes with his icy blue stare. "If you care about Tristan at all, even a little bit, then I beseech you to do everything you can to help me."

"I will," I said after a moment.

After a pause, Luca told me where everyone would be, then he left, closing the glass doors behind him. As soon as he was gone, I returned to Logan's bedside and gave him a smile. "Sorry. Do you want soup or the sandwich? Or both?"

Logan reached across with his good arm and grabbed my hand, his fingers digging into my palm, and I knew what was coming. We hadn't really had a chance to talk alone since he'd woken up.

"Seriously, Luni? You've got us mixed up with the fucking mafia?"

I started to shake my head, but then stopped. My brother wasn't stupid. "I didn't mean to."

"We need to get the hell out of here. I know someone from school whose father is mafia. I've heard stories, Luni. We need to go before we know too much. Go back to my dorm or the apartment or a hotel or *something*. This isn't a fucking joke. I mean, *look* at me. These people are fucking dangerous."

I squeezed his hand. "I know what kind of people they are, but they're the only thing keeping us safe right now with Gino still out there." I refused to call him our father out loud. No father would do the things to us that he had. "They can protect us here." That was all true, but would I run if I could? Honestly, I didn't know. I hadn't had the energy to think about anything other than Logan getting well.

"I don't trust them," Logan insisted. "Especially not that Tristan guy. I don't like the way he looks at you..."

"Shh, it's okay," I soothed, brushing the hair back from his forehead like I used to do when he was little. "I'll keep you safe, I promise. We just need to lay low here a little longer. Once they find Gino, this will all be over, and we can go back to our normal lives." Whatever that may be.

"Stop it." He let go of my hand. "I'm not a fucking child anymore. I can walk. We need to go, and we need to do it now."

"We can't just leave, Logan."

"Why the hell not?"

"Because there are guards. And cameras."

He stared over at me in disbelief. "So, we're prisoners?"

I shook my head. "No."

"Then why can't we leave?"

I took a deep breath. "Logan, have I ever let anything happen to you?"

"This isn't the same, Luni."

"Have I?" I insisted.

He glanced at me out of the corner of his eye. "No."

"And I won't let anything happen to you now. You just have to trust me."

Logan didn't look convinced, but eventually, he sank back against the pillows with an impatient sigh. I hated seeing him so shaken and scared, but on this point, I knew I was right. Honestly, I didn't know if Luca would allow Logan to leave, but I did know Tristan would throw me back in his cell the moment I tried. I was kind of surprised he hadn't already. It made me nervous, and a little bit scared.

But all of that aside, it was true. Gino would find us again if we left the safety of Luca's. And I preferred to never see that motherfucker again.

I brought his tray to him, then leaned over and kissed his forehead. "Eat your lunch. I'll be back as soon as I can."

Rubbing my fingertips together nervously, I left him to it and made my way across the house to face the family, praying this nightmare would be over soon.

CHAPTER 10

Luna

"Please, come in and make yourselves comfortable," Luca said as everyone arrived, gesturing to the large formal dining room. The capos filed in, greeting him with respect and taking their seats around the table.

I hesitated in the doorway, my stomach churning as I watched the table fill up. A few of the men I recognized from the club, but not as many as I'd feared. Good. Maybe they'd actually take me somewhat seriously.

A large, warm hand touched my lower back, and when I looked up I was surprised to find Tristan beside me.

"You don't have to do this, Luna," he murmured.

I took a deep breath, trying to calm my racing heart. "No, I want to. If it'll help you find Gino, I'll do what I can." My voice sounded steadier than I felt. The thought of facing the capos, the men who knew my father, made my insides twist in knots. But I had to be strong. For Logan. For myself. And for the damaged man standing beside me.

"You understand that if we find him, he'll be dead as soon as Luca gets all the information out of him that he needs."

"Yes," I told him. "I understand." And I did. If Luca didn't kill him, Tristan would.

His dark eyes searched my face for a long moment, and then he gave me a nod before leaving me standing there in the doorway and making his way to his place behind Luca's chair.

Enzo came in then and guided me to a chair by the windows near Luca. I sat, my hands twisting in my lap as Lisa bustled in and out, setting out bowls of bread and plates of pasta in front of the guests and filling their glasses with water and red wine. As everyone caught up with business, I pushed my food around on my plate, feeling Tristan's constant stare as he watched me.

The men at the table also openly stared at me, some with appreciation, some not, but no one was rude enough to question why I was at the table. They probably assumed I was Luca's new side piece since Veda wasn't here.

Luca waited until pleasantries had been exchanged and everyone had eaten some of their meal before leaning forward, his elbows on the table and his fingers laced together. "Thank you all for coming on such short notice.

We have an urgent situation to discuss." He waited until everyone was paying attention. "As I'm sure you've noticed, Gino Ricci is not here."

There were some murmurs around the table.

"He's not here because he's in hiding. I've had my suspicions for quite a long time, however yesterday I saw the proof with my own eyes. Gino is working with the Bratva."

"I don't believe it!" The shout came from the end of the table. A man around Gino's age threw down his napkin. "Where is your proof?"

Luca cocked his head at the outburst, and a chill ran down my spine as he said, "The fact that I saw them with my own eyes isn't enough for you? Are you saying I'm lying?"

The older man was red in the face, but he backed down when everyone turned to look at him. "Of course not, Luca. I apologize."

"Should we be speaking of this right now?" another man across the table asked, lifting his chin toward me.

Luca sat back in his chair. "This is Luna. She's Gino's daughter."

Another rumble of murmurs exploded around the table.

"I thought both of the children died with their mother?" someone said.

"That is just one of the many lies Gino has told us," Luca told them. "The children were put up for adoption, and you can see by looking at her, Luna is the image of her mother. Her brother, Logan, is currently recuperating from *his* reunion with their father here in my home."

The looks I received now were more curious than lewd.

"Luna is here because she recently stayed with her father after he found her in the club where she worked, and she has some interesting things to say." He looked to me. "Luna, please tell everyone about how you found your father again and what it was like living with him. As much as you can remember."

I glanced at Tristan, who hadn't taken his eyes from me. Of course, Luca knew what my role was—and what he'd done to me—at Gino's before Tristan took me out of there.

I swallowed hard, my mouth dry. Haltingly at first, I began to recount the events of the past few weeks—seeing Gino where I worked, the poker games, how I got in on them, our bet, how he'd starved me, how he would get drunk and confuse me with my mother. I didn't go into details about the rapes, but I did tell them it always happened when he was drinking. Lastly, I told them how he came into my room with a gun, ready to kill the both of us. And how Tristan had brought me here.

My voice shook as I described how Gino had gone after Logan, and how I'd found him beaten and tied up. I skipped over the parts of the story where Tristan was involved. Again, it wasn't my story to tell.

The capos listened in grim silence, their faces darkening with each revelation. When I finished, Luca sat back, rubbing a hand over his mouth before he spoke. "If what his own daughter just told you isn't enough, we've suspected for a while now that Gino has been working with the Russians. Not long ago, I gave them all a little warning, one Gino and the Russians chose to ignore. Yesterday, however, we got our proof. Enzo, Tristan, and I saw Gino with them. They opened fire on us." He paused. "Gino needs to be taken care of."

"I agree," one of the capos growled. "This cannot stand. Gino's a traitor to you and to the family. He must be dealt with."

Murmurs of assent echoed around the table. Luca met the gaze of every man there. "I want eyes on every street corner, every hole in the wall Gino might scurry to. We need to find him, and we need to end whatever alliance he has with the Russians. "

"God only knows what kind of information he's giving them, or what he's promised them," the man across from me said.

"That's something I intend to find out," Luca promised. Then he stood and gave me a nod. A sign that it was time for me to go and let the boys talk. "Thank you, Luna. I know that wasn't easy for you."

"You're welcome," I told him. I felt numb as I was dismissed from the room, the capos' dark mutterings and Tristan's heavy gaze following me.

I made my way back to Logan's room, my mind whirling. I'd just betrayed my own father, condemned him to death. But what choice did I have? He was who he was, and other than taking care of Logan's school costs, he'd never done anything to earn my loyalty, and he'd never stop coming after us. If for no other reason than some sick need for revenge.

I pushed open the door to Logan's room and found him sitting up in bed, his face pale and his lunch untouched in front of him. "What happened?" he demanded.

I sank into the chair near him, rubbing my face with both hands. "They just wanted to know about Gino," I said. "I told them everything." Well, not everything, but enough.

He was quiet for a long time. "Is it true? What he told me? Did you fuck him? Our own father?"

Shame washed over me. "I didn't know he was our father then, and it's not like I had a choice."

"He told me you were a stripper, and a whore." There was no disgust in my brother's voice, just curiosity.

Shrugging, I said, "The stripping part is true. That's how I made enough money to give us a place to live and to help you pay for school."

"I could've helped, Luni. I could've gotten a job."

I smiled. "It wouldn't have been enough. Besides, I don't mind dancing. I've never been shy about my body, and I won't be able to do it forever. Plus, the club I worked at takes really good care of me and all the girls who work there."

My brother was quiet for a long moment, studying my face. I waited for his judgment, but I should've known that wasn't the kind of man he was, because it never came. "Do you think they'll find him?"

"I don't know," I admitted. "But they're going to try."

He nodded, his jaw tight. "Good. I hope they do. And I hope they make him pay for what he did to you."

I squeezed his hand, grateful that we still had each other. "Me too," I whispered.

A soft knock sounded on the door, and I turned to see Tristan standing there, his dark eyes unreadable. "Can I speak with you for a moment?" he asked.

I met Logan's gaze. He shook his head slightly. "I'll be right back," I promised, rising to my feet.

I followed Tristan out into the great room, my skin tingling with nervous energy. He led me away from the doors and out of my brother's earshot before stopping and turning to face me.

"I just wanted to check on you," he said, his voice low.

I met his eyes, trying to appear steadier than I felt. "I'm fine," I told him. I swallowed hard, my heart racing. "Tristan, I..." I trailed off into silence, not knowing what to say.

His dark eyes bored into mine with an intensity that made my pulse race. "I don't like you being here."

I frowned. "At Luca's?"

"Yes." He reached out, gently brushing a strand of hair back from my face, his fingertips grazing my cheek.

I shivered at his touch. "I'd think the home of the mafia boss would be a pretty safe place to hang out."

"It is."

"Then I don't understand."

His hand fell back to his side as his eyes darkened. "Neither do I."

I couldn't tear my eyes away from him. "What don't you understand?"

"When does the wanting stop, Luna?" he whispered. "Will I ever be able to get you the fuck out of my head?"

I stared up at him in surprise, my pulse pounding in my ears. This dangerous, enigmatic man had turned my world upside down from the moment he entered my life. And now here he was, laying his soul bare before me.

"Tristan..." I breathed.

He cupped my face in his large hands, his eyes intense on mine and his thumbs stroking my cheekbones. "Tell me you feel it too, *bambolina*. Tell me it's not just me."

I opened my mouth to respond, my heart hammering against my ribcage. But before I could get a word out, he wrapped his fists in my hair and kissed me.

CHAPTER 11

Tristan

I felt her need for me in the way her body surged into mine, even as I sensed her hesitation under my lips, and both set my blood on fire. Her hands flew to my chest, searing my mutilated skin right through the thin material of my black dress shirt. Her fingers curled into fists, gripping my shirt to keep me close as she tried to push me away, her lips parting on a moan of denial as she let me in.

A shudder ran through my body. It had been so long since I tasted her.

I wanted to rip off our clothes and bury myself so deep inside her she would taste it when I came. But now was not the time or the place.

With a ragged groan, I bit her bottom lip in frustration, the coppery taste of her blood sweet on my tongue as I allowed her to push me away.

My lungs ached for air as Luna broke the kiss and backed away from me, her blue eyes wide with hunger and uncertainty. The rise and fall of her chest matched my own ragged breaths, and I could sense the war raging within her—the desire to give in to me battling against her instinct to flee—because it matched my own.

I took a step toward her, my body drawn to hers, craving her touch, her taste, her everything. But I forced myself to stop, to remain still, though every fiber of my being screamed at me to close the distance between us and claim what was mine.

I watched as she gingerly touched the wound on her lip, her eyes wide in disbelief as she stared down at the drops of blood.

Without a second thought, I reached out and took her hand in mine, drawing her fingers to my mouth. Slowly, deliberately, I sucked each one clean, savoring the taste of her. The near animalistic urge to claim her, to make her mine, surged through me once more. I wanted nothing more than to crush my lips against hers again, to devour her until there was nothing but my name on her tongue.

But when I bent to take her mouth again, she jerked her hand from my grip and put more distance between us. "Stop."

I hesitated, but only for a moment.

"NO," she said, turning her face away.

I drew back, my eyes devouring her perfect features.

"I'm not coming with you," she told me. "If that's why you're here. I'm not going back to that cell, Tristan."

"Luna..." Instead of what I was about to say, my fists tightened at my sides.

Isn't this what you want? For your life to go back to normal?

Yes.

NO.

I need to let her go. As soon as her brother is able, they'll be gone, and I'll never have to see her again.

But she's MINE.

"What's between us is..." She looked around, trying to find the words in the paintings hanging on the wall. "It's powerful," she finally finished. "And I know I was the first person you'd ever been with freely, so I'm sure for you it seems like no one else will ever be able to take my place, but there are a lot of other women out there, Tristan, who would happily cut off their arm to be with a man like you and live in this world."

"I don't want someone else. I want you. It's only you, Luna." My voice was strained as the truth forced its way out. This world, my world, wasn't safe for her, and she was right; she'd be better off without me. But I would never want another woman.

She shook her head vehemently, then lifted her chin. "No, Tristan. I know what you want, and it's not happening. I'm staying here with Logan. And when he's well enough to leave and Gino has been taken care of, I'm going with my brother." She glanced toward the dining room where the meeting was finishing up.

I cocked my head. "Do you think they will stop me? Do you think anyone here will stop me if I throw you over my shoulder and take you with me?"

"No," she conceded after a pause. "But I'm asking you not to. I don't want to be in your prison. I don't want to be with you."

She was lying. At least about the second part. She did want to be with me. She loved it when I fucked her.

Even knowing it wasn't true, hearing her say those words felt like she was twisting a knife in my gut. After all this time, and everything that had happened between us, she still saw me as nothing but her captor.

As she backed away, I stalked after her, matching every step. But I couldn't have said if it was to throw her against the wall and kiss her until she admitted to her lies, or to throw her out of the house and force myself to forget she ever existed.

Before I could reach her, the dining room doors swung open, and the capos strode out, their faces grim. Despite what I'd just told her, I froze, not wanting to make a scene where I'd have to explain myself or my actions to them.

Luna seized the opportunity to dart back into Logan's room.

Instinctually, I moved to go after her, but Luca suddenly appeared in front of me. "Tristan, let her go to her brother," he ordered. *"Tristan."*

His tone had a sharp edge to it, demanding my full attention, and I responded automatically, forcing my eyes from the doorway where she'd disappeared. I met his stern gaze, noting the hint of warning there, the silent command to let Luna be for now. With every cell in my body screaming at me not to allow her to leave my sight, I battled the overwhelming compulsion to chase after her. But I couldn't disobey him, especially not in front of the other capos.

Luca met my gaze unflinchingly. "She'll be safe here. I swear it to you. Right now, I need you to go with Enzo."

Letting Luna out of my sight went against every instinct I had. And a part of me—the part that was raised on brutality and molded by violence—wanted to reach out and seize control of everything around me. To tear apart anyone who stood between me and Luna with my bare hands, if necessary. Including Luca.

The other part wished I'd never gone to her window.

I took a deep breath, trying to calm myself. My mind told me that Luna was safer here at Luca's than she would be at my house. Though I had my cell and I preferred her contained, the lake house boasted a safe room downstairs that was practically a fortress. Built into the side of the cliff, it was virtually impenetrable to any outside threats. If anything happened, she'd be protected by layers of steel and concrete. No one would be able to get to her.

Still, that knowledge did little to soothe the clawing unease in my gut at letting her out of my sight, even for a moment. Every instinct roared at me to keep her close, to not let her stray from my watchful gaze. Gritting my teeth and curling my hands into fists, I fought the overwhelming urge to go after her, but in the end, my training overrode my own needs.

With a snarl of frustration, I stalked off, my body burning with lust, and a deep ache in my chest.

Enzo waited for me near the front door, and I headed toward him, my palms damp and my mind reeling. The taste of Luna's blood lingered on my tongue, and I could still feel the silk of her hair in my hands.

He studied me as I approached. "You good, T?"

I nodded once. "Where are we going?"

"We're gonna go hit a few places. See if anyone's seen Gino. And there's a pickup tonight Luca wants us to be there for."

I nodded, following him outside. The crisp air did little to soothe the fire burning inside of me or calm the buzzing in my veins.

Enzo interrupted my thoughts of Luna. "Before we leave, I have to ask. If we happen to find Gino, and it's just you and me, are you gonna be okay with that?"

Looking up from the ground, I found him directly in front of me where he'd stopped near the passenger side door of my SUV. "I think so." It was the best I could give him.

I felt him studying me through the dark lenses of his glasses. "If we do happen to get a lead, and if for any reason at all your head's not in the game, you need to tell me. *Comprendere?*"

He was right. Only two people in this world were capable of throwing me off balance, and Gino was one of them. "I will," I promised.

His hard stare burned through me, and then he opened the door and got in.

I slid into the driver's seat, trying to shove my encounter with Luna into a tiny compartment of my mind where I could pull it out and relive it later. Right now, I needed to have my head on straight like Enzo said. Gino was out there somewhere, and I needed to find him, and I couldn't let him get to me. I couldn't endanger Enzo's life like that.

Funny how I was willing enough to obey Luca's orders to let Gino live when it was just about me. By the time I was put into Luca's service, the sight of Gino had barely gotten a reaction out of me. And the more time that went on, the more confident I felt that he couldn't touch me anymore. I'd taken my memories from my time with him and shoved them so deep it was like it never happened. At least, until something triggered me. But now that Luna was involved...yeah, I didn't know that it would be a good thing if I found him first this time.

As I pulled out of the driveway, Enzo glanced over at me. "You sure you're good, T?"

I nodded, my grip tightening on the steering wheel. "I'm fine."

But I wasn't fine. Not really. Luna's words kept echoing in my head.

I don't want to be with you.

I shook my head, trying to clear my thoughts.

"Seriously, T, you can turn around. You don't have to do this right now. I can take one of the other guys."

"I said I'm good."

I could tell he didn't believe me, but he didn't push the matter any farther.

I pulled onto the road, my mind a tangled mess. Part of me wanted to turn the car around, march back into that house, and take Luna with me, consequences be damned. But the rational part of my brain knew I couldn't do that. Not now. I had a job to do.

But I felt like I was being torn in two, caught between my duty and my desire. Between what I knew I had to do and what every fiber of my being was screaming at me to do. And I didn't know how much longer I could keep fighting it.

And as we drove on into the night, I couldn't shake the feeling that everything was about to change. That the fragile balance I'd been clinging to was about to shatter into a million pieces.

And I didn't know if I'd be able to put myself back together again.

CHAPTER 12

Luna

I sat by Logan's bedside, my mind a tempest of conflicting emotions as my brother's questions hung heavy in the air, demanding answers I wasn't sure I could give.

"Just tell me how you got mixed up with these guys, Luni," Logan said. "How the hell did you end up with *him*?"

It was like he was afraid to say Tristan's name for fear he'd suddenly appear. "I told you. Tristan brought me here from Gino's when he found out I was actually his daughter."

"You didn't know him before that?"

I thought back to those nights Tristan snuck into my room. The way he'd touched me, and still did, like I was something precious, something owned. Like he could barely control his hunger for me. How he wouldn't let me numb myself. Or starve.

But I didn't want to tell my brother all of that. Those memories were mine, and they were private. "Not before I met him at the wedding, like I told you, and I'd seen him when he came to Gino's with Luca."

"And you've been here all this time? With him?"

"Well, at his house down the road, yes. Until you—well, Gino—texted me."

He started pushing himself up on the pillows and I rushed over to help him so he wouldn't hurt his ribs. Swinging his legs over the side of his bed, he sat still for a few seconds, catching his breath.

"I just don't understand why you'd throw away your life on a poker game."

How to explain to him that I didn't know any other way to live? First with our foster father, then dancing in the clubs, and finally with Gino. Trading my body for money, for his safety, was all I knew how to do. "I was just trying to survive," I told him, choosing my words carefully. "And to get the money to help you pay off your school."

"I should've never gone to college. Or I should've studied harder so I could've gotten more grants."

I sat down on the bed beside him. "It's not your fault, Logan. And I want you in school. You're going to be a great nurse."

He was quiet for a minute, then he asked, "Did Mr. Phillips..." He sniffed, his good eye cutting to me before staring straight ahead. "Did he do things to you?"

I tried to play it off. "Why would you ask that?"

Logan glanced at me, then away. "I saw the way he looked at you, Luni. I was young, but I wasn't stupid."

Guess I wasn't as good at hiding things from my little brother as I'd thought. "Well, he also taught me how to play poker," I told him without answering his question. "I'm really good at it. I won so much money before I played Gino that we would've been comfortable for a long time."

"You should've quit while you were ahead."

I laughed. "Yeah."

"So what about this Tristan guy?" he asked when we fell quiet again. "What's he to you?"

The smile slipped from my face. "I'm not really sure," I told him honestly.

"He doesn't seem particularly...warm," he finished.

I didn't laugh that time. "He's been through a lot, Logan. And it's made him the way he is. Try not to judge him too harshly, okay?"

"Like what?"

I rubbed my forehead. "Well, he was raised to be one of Luca's guards. And from what I've heard, it was a horrifying way for a little boy to grow up. Now, protecting Luca is the only reason he has for living."

"Until you."

Giving him a small smile, I said, "I guess? Maybe. He's having a hard time dealing with some stuff right now. And I am, too. I don't think this life is one I want to live. And I don't want you anywhere near it."

"So why don't you just break it off with him?" he asked. "And don't tell me 'it's complicated.'"

I took a second to think about my answer. "Because of how he was raised, Tristan had..." How to explain a man as enigmatic as him? "...shut down," I finished. "He has a hard time understanding emotions, and I don't think he really feels that many. But he put his life in danger for me, to keep me safe, and I don't know. I feel like I owe him some grace for that." And probably a little more gratitude than I'd shown him so far.

"So you're telling me you're dating a psychopath?"

I shook my head. "I don't think it's that bad."

Logan's brow furrowed, concern etched across his features. I knew he couldn't understand the inexplicable pull I felt toward Tristan, the way my body responded to his touch despite the warning bells in my head. And I wasn't about to try to explain it to him.

"I know it doesn't make sense," I admitted. "But there's a connection between us, something I can't explain." Something I didn't even have the words for.

I fell silent then, the weight of my confession hanging in the air. Logan reached for my hand, and I gave his a squeeze. "How about a shower and a change of clothes?"

"That would be great. But you're not helping me, Luni."

"I'm your sister!" I laughed.

"And I'm twenty-two, which is way too old for you to see me naked."

"You'll always be little to me."

Carefully sliding off the bed, he gave me a grin that I was sure made all the girls' hearts flutter. "I ain't so little anymore, sis."

"Ew, Logan." Slapping him on the shoulder, I made sure he was steady on his feet before we continued to the gym. Veda told me there was a shower in there and she'd left some clean clothes for Logan on the counter.

"I still can't get over this house," he told me as we walked through the great room to the opposite hallway.

I looked up at the ceiling, two floors up. "Right?"

"Have you seen all of it?"

"Not much more than you. Hopefully, Veda gave me good directions."

Once we got to the gym, I helped him cover his arm brace. "Take your time. And if you need me, just yell. I'll be right out here," I told him before leaving him alone.

"I'll be fine, Luni. Stop worrying about me."

I sank down onto one of the benches in the gym, letting out a heavy sigh as I listened to the water running in the other room. Finally, I had a moment to myself, a chance to sort through the tangled web of thoughts and emotions swirling inside my head.

Logan was right, of course. I knew deep down that I needed to put some distance between Tristan and myself. It was the logical thing to do, the smart thing to do. But even as I sat there, trying to convince myself that leaving was the only option, I couldn't ignore the dull ache that settled in my chest at the thought of walking away from him.

It didn't make any sense. I couldn't understand why the idea of leaving behind the man who'd kept me captive in a cell filled me with such a profound sense of loss, a hollow emptiness that threatened to swallow me whole. I knew I should want to escape, to run as far away from him as I could get... but I didn't. Despite everything, some small, irrational part of me wanted to stay.

I stared at myself in the wall of mirrors, studying the swollen scrape on my face. Funny, I still looked like the same girl who danced topless in the club, her only focus collecting as much cash as possible from the men watching her, but I didn't feel like that girl anymore. I wasn't sure how to explain it. I was just...different.

I touched the small wound on my lip and thought about the way Tristan had kissed me with such desperation, like he was afraid I'd disappear if he let go. The way he'd held me close, his body solid and warm and large against mine. Protective. And for a moment, I'd felt safe in a way I never had before.

But then I shook my head, trying to clear the memories. I couldn't let myself get caught up in him and the way he made me feel. I had to be strong, for Logan's sake, if not my own.

Yet even as I told myself that, I couldn't ignore the part of me that wanted to stay, that craved his touch and the way he looked at me like I was the only thing that mattered in his life.

I'd never mattered that much to anyone. Not even my brother.

I didn't understand it, this pull he had on me. And I hated the way it made me question everything I thought I knew.

It would be good for me to get away from him, to clear my head and get my life back on track. I wasn't lying when I'd said I didn't want this life. I didn't want to be the mistress of a mafia man. I'd lived my entire life in a body that was the property of men in one way or the other. So no, even if Gino was gone, I didn't want this life.

I wanted to be free.

Even if the thought of leaving, of never seeing him again, made my heart clench in a way I didn't want to examine too closely.

THE NEXT FEW days passed in a blur as Logan continued to heal. I spent most of my time by his side, making sure he was comfortable and had everything he needed. Veda was a godsend, always there with a kind word or a helping hand. And Lisa kept us well fed.

As Logan grew stronger, he started wandering around the house, usually with Enzo as a tour guide, and I found myself with more time to think. And the more I thought, the more I realized that we couldn't stay here. I didn't like him spending so much time with Enzo, and I didn't want to overstay our welcome. So far, Luca hadn't asked for anything in return for his kindness, and maybe he never would. But I didn't want to take that chance.

I hadn't seen Tristan since the day of the meeting with the capos.

I tried not to think about that.

It wasn't that I didn't care for him. I did, more than I wanted to admit. But I was done trading my body and my freedom for survival. Logan told me he had a little money stashed away that he hadn't used for living expenses. It was enough for us to get by for a short time until I could find a respectable job in a restaurant or something. I wasn't expecting to see the money I'd lost to Gino ever again, but that was okay. We wouldn't have an easy life, but we'd have each other, and we'd get by.

I wanted a life of my own, one where I was free to make my own choices and live on my own terms. And as much as it pained me to admit it, I knew I couldn't have that with Tristan.

So I made a decision. I would go see him one last time to thank him for everything he'd done for me. And then I would tell him that I was leaving.

My heart clenched at the thought of walking away from him, but I knew it was the right thing to do. For both of us. Logan and I would leave tomorrow and take an Uber back to his dorms, get Logan's car, and drive until we found somewhere where Gino wouldn't find us. My brother could transfer schools. Maybe not at first, but as soon as we were stable somewhere.

He'd argued with me about that. He wanted to work and help support us, and I'd agreed for the short term. But I was determined that he finish his schooling.

I waited until Logan was busy hanging out in the kitchen with Lisa, and then I slipped out of the house.

Taking a deep breath of the crisp morning air, I started walking, my feet carrying me down the drive to Tristan's.

As I approached the house, I hesitated. Maybe it would be better if I left without telling him. Or wait for him to come to Luca's before I said anything.

I'll always come for you.

This was stupid. I didn't know how he was going to react. Maybe I'd just tell him thank you and skip the part about leaving. That way I'd have said what I came here to say, but he'd have no reason to panic and throw me back in the cell.

Maybe being at Luca's these last few days had given me too much confidence. And maybe, Tristan wouldn't care at all. Maybe I'd proven to be more trouble than I was worth.

These thoughts spun around in my head as I stood there, undecided. What was the real reason I was here? Was it to thank him? Or because I missed him?

I was about to turn around and go back to Luca's when the door opened and Tristan stood in the doorway. My eyes roamed down his body, taking in the hard muscle beneath the black suit, and a burning ache began deep in my lower belly.

And when my eyes returned to his face, the hunger and pain in his eyes made my knees go weak.

Oh, god.

CHAPTER 13

Tristan

Luna stood in my doorway, her face a mix of uncertainty and desire. I drank in the sight of her, the curves of her body, the way her hair fell around her shoulders. The swelling on her face had gone down, the scrapes scabbed over. She was exquisite. My heart raced and my cock swelled just looking at her. It had only been a few days, but it felt like an eternity since I'd seen her.

I stepped back, inviting her inside. She hesitated for a moment before crossing the threshold and standing awkwardly in the kitchen. The click of the door closing behind her echoed in the silence as I drank her in, from her dark hair to her sneakers. She was wearing her own jeans, clean now, but the pink T-shirt was something I'd seen Veda wearing.

"I came to say thank you," she said quietly. "For everything you've done for me. And for Logan."

I cocked my head, watching her.

"You kept me safe from Gino, and came after me when I was stupid enough to fall for his games, and I just wanted you to know that it means a lot to me. And I appreciate it."

Why did I get the feeling that she was trying to tell me goodbye?

I moved closer, crowding her space until her back was against the wall. "Is that the only reason you're here, *bambolina?*"

Her breath hitched and her pulse fluttered wildly at the base of her throat. "I..." Blue eyes flew to mine and held. "I don't know."

"I think you do." I brushed my knuckles along her injured cheek, relishing the way she shivered at my touch. "I think you missed me."

She swallowed hard. "Tristan, I can't... We can't..."

"Can't what? Can't admit how much you want me? How much you crave my touch?" I leaned in, my lips a hairsbreadth from hers. "Tell me you don't want this, Luna. Tell me to stop." I wouldn't. Because holy fuck, there was a buzzing along the surface of my skin. I wanted her hands on me again. Wanted to feel her soft, pale skin pressed against mine until the revulsion faded and there was only hunger.

For a long moment, she stared at me, chest heaving, eyes dark with need. Then she surged forward, crashing her mouth against mine in a heated kiss. I groaned, tangling my fingers in her hair as I claimed her mouth, our tongues dueling for dominance.

She flattened her palms against my chest, and I jerked as a raw, keening sound tore from my throat, forcing myself to stay where I was.

Luna stiffened.

"Touch me," I begged her against her soft lips. *"Please."* I wanted her hands on me. I dreamed of her touch, waking up in the middle of the night covered in sweat with an aching erection and the cold fingers of terror sliding down my spine.

Only to find myself alone.

Always alone.

Slowly, she wrapped her arms around my neck, pressing the length of her body against mine, and I shuddered. My hands gripped her hips, pulling her closer as I deepened the kiss. I couldn't get enough of her. The taste of her mouth. The scent of her skin and hair. The sweet sound of her moans. She consumed me, filling my senses until there was nothing but Luna.

I broke away from her mouth to trail kisses along her jaw, down the column of her throat. She tipped her head back with a breathy moan, and I nipped at her pulse point, soothing the sting with my tongue. My hands slid beneath her shirt, skating over the smooth skin of her back, and she arched into me with a gasp.

"Tristan," she whispered, and I tightened my grip on her, my name on her lips driving me insane.

I lifted my head to meet her gaze, and the heat in her eyes nearly undid me. I wanted to take her right there against the wall, to bury myself deep inside her and never let her go. But I forced myself to slow down, to savor every moment. To drown in her.

I pulled her shirt over her head and tossed it aside, my eyes devouring the sight of her in a lacy black bra. She was fucking perfect, all creamy skin and soft curves, and I couldn't resist the urge to touch her. I cupped her breasts, feeling the weight of them in my palms, and she let out a soft whimper.

"So beautiful," I murmured, brushing my thumbs over her nipples through the thin fabric. They hardened beneath my touch, and she shivered.

I wanted to take my time with her, to worship every inch of her body until she was trembling and begging for more. But the need thrumming through my veins was too intense, too all-consuming. I needed her now, needed to be inside her, to claim her as mine.

I reached for the button of her jeans, but she caught my wrist, stilling my movements.

I looked up at her, a question in my eyes. "Do *not* deny me now, Luna."

"Tristan..." She said nothing else, and I couldn't read her emotions in her eyes or her expression. There was too much confusion.

With a growl, I scooped her up into my arms and carried her down the hall to my bedroom, kicking the door shut behind us. I laid her down on the bed and stood back, drinking in the sight of her sprawled out before me like an offering from the gods.

She didn't try to get up. Didn't try to leave.

Mine. She was mine.

Without thinking about the bright light streaming in through the windows, I stripped off my jacket and let it fall to the floor, my eyes never leaving hers. Removing my side holster, I laid that and my Glock on the nightstand. Then I kicked off my shoes and removed the rest of my clothing. She watched me with a mix of hunger and trepidation, her teeth worrying at her lower lip. I could see the desire warring with uncertainty in her eyes, the same things that were fighting inside of me. But I didn't care. I needed her too damn much to stop now.

When I was fully nude, I finished undressing her, dropping kisses along every inch of skin that was revealed to me.

I crawled onto the bed, hovering over her, enjoying the way she trembled beneath me. Lowering my head, I pressed a kiss to the hollow of her throat, feeling her pulse jump beneath my lips. She gasped, her fingers digging into my scalp as I nipped and licked my way lower, over the swell of her breasts. They were so perfect. Round and full with dusky nipples that hardened in my mouth. I flicked my tongue over one peak, and she cried out, arching into me.

"Tristan, please..." Her voice was breathy, needy, and it only fueled the fire raging inside me.

I moved lower, pressing open-mouthed kisses down the soft curve of her stomach, running my tongue up the inside of her thigh until her hips lifted off the bed. Slowly, I worked my way up, my teeth nipping at the soft skin of her inner thighs. When I reached her pussy, I paused, breathing in the heady scent of her arousal.

"You're so wet for me, *bambolina*," I murmured, my voice rough with desire. "I can't wait to taste you."

She whimpered, widening her legs as her hips writhed on the bed in silent invitation. I didn't need any further encouragement. I lowered my head, swiping my tongue through her slick folds, and she cried out, her fingers tightening in my hair.

She tasted like heaven, sweet and tangy, and I groaned against her flesh. I found the spot on her clit that drove her crazy, and licked and sucked until her moans filled the room. Then I slid two fingers inside her, feeling her tight heat clench around me, and I nearly came undone.

"Tristan, oh god..." She was panting now, her hips rocking against my face as I drove her closer to the edge. "Please..."

Sliding my fingers in and out in a quick, steady rhythm, I pressed against her lower belly with my free hand, holding her still as I devoured her in the most intimate way. I wanted to taste her to cum on my tongue. Wanted to feel her lose control. This. This is what I craved. Always. To play her like an instrument until everything she felt, the pleasure, the pain, was because of me.

Just me and Luna, until the world around us didn't exist anymore.

She stiffened on the bed, and I growled deep in my throat, knowing she was close. So fucking close. My cock grew painfully hard, and I rolled my hips into the bed, unable to help myself. Sucking her clit into my mouth, I flicked it gently with my tongue and pressed my fingers deep inside of her, curling them forward the way she liked until she arched off the bed, crying out hoarsely as she orgasmed so hard her womb contracted beneath my hand and she drenched my fingers.

Pulling my fingers out of her cunt, I sucked them clean as she watched me with hooded eyes, her chest rising and falling with rapid breaths. Then I put my mouth back on her, ignoring her half-hearted protests, working her up slowly until she was once again squirming beneath me.

Only then did I rise over her and position my throbbing cock at her entrance. "Look at me, Luna," I demanded, my voice rough with need.

She opened her eyes.

"I missed you. The taste of you. The feel of you."

She whimpered, then cried out as I pushed inside of her. I groaned as her hot, wet heat tightened around me. Pulling out slightly, I thrusted in again until she took all of me deep inside of her.

Her arms wrapped around my ribcage, and her fingernails dug into my lower back. Her legs covered mine. The sensation of her smooth skin against my scars was both overwhelming and not enough. Luna was everywhere. All around me. And for a moment I couldn't do anything but breathe through it, until with a last shuddering breath, I began to move.

I wanted to take my time, but I only made it through a few long strokes at that pace. Sliding one arm underneath her, I fucked her hard and fast, reveling in the sounds she made. In the way she met me stroke for stroke, urging me on with her grip on my hips.

And when I couldn't get deep enough, I rolled over onto my back, taking her with me. She sat up and I slid even deeper inside of her. My grip tightened on her hips, hard enough to bruise. She gasped, but didn't pull away, instead rocking against me more urgently.

"You're mine," I snarled. Reaching up, I grabbed her around the neck and pulled her mouth down, capturing her mouth in a brutal kiss. "Say it. Say you belong to me."

Tears leaked from the corners of her eyes. "I belong to you," she choked out. "I'm yours, Tristan."

My orgasm shot up my shaft and I came hard, her capitulation the most beautifully terrifying thing I'd ever heard.

My heart was still racing as I pulled away from Luna and sat up on the side of the bed, my breathing ragged. The intoxicating taste of her still lingered on my lips. I'd never felt anything like this—a gnawing hunger, yes, but also a dizzying vulnerability that made me want to run and never look back.

I clenched my fists, welcoming the bite of pain as my nails dug into my palms. Pain was familiar, pain made sense. Not like these other feelings, these dangerous cracks in the armor I'd spent years building around myself. Feelings were a weakness I couldn't afford, not with my job.

"Tristan?" Luna came to sit beside me, pulling the sheet over her nudity. She put a hand on my arm, and I recoiled as if burned.

Pulling her hand back, she stared at me in confusion.

I schooled my features into a cold mask, my jaw tight. There was no room for softness in my life. For compassion. No place for the bewildering warmth she stirred in me. I thought that once I'd satisfied my curiosity about her, once I knew that Gino wouldn't hurt anyone else, I would fixate on something else, just like I always did.

But I was starting to see that wasn't the case with her. Instead of fading, my fixation was turning into an all-consuming obsession that only grew stronger the longer she was around. And that was dangerous for a man like me.

I was forgetting that I wasn't a man. I was a bullet shield for Luca, hardened by blood and violence. That was all. I couldn't keep her. I didn't need her.

Even if some traitorous part of me whispered that I did.

CHAPTER 14

Tristan

Grabbing everything except my jacket and gun, I went into the bathroom. I didn't wash, preferring to leave her scent on my skin even though I knew I shouldn't. When I was once again clothed, I came back into the bedroom to find Luna had also gotten dressed.

I took a deep breath before turning to face her. She sat on the edge of my bed, her expression open and expectant. I knew it was time to come clean about my past, no matter how dark that truth might be.

"There's something I need to tell you," I said reluctantly, my voice barely above a whisper.

She waited, her body suddenly tense, as if she knew what I was about to say would change everything.

I moved to stand before her, every muscle in my body wound tight. "You know that in my work, there are times when I have to do things normal people would never have to do. People like you and your brother."

"This is about the photo of me and my mother," she guessed. I tried to read her face, to get a feel for what was going through her head, but her expression was carefully neutral. I fucking hated it when she did that. When she shut me out like I was one of her Johns.

I didn't say anything about her snooping around my office. What would be the point now? Instead, I told her what she was too afraid to ask me. "When I was twenty-two, I was given my first solitary job." I glanced at the floor, unable to hold her gaze as I pulled the memories from their box. "Luigi, Luca's father, ordered me to take care of a problem. A loose end."

I glanced up at her. She hadn't moved a muscle. Did she know what I was about to tell her? "That loose end was your mother."

Her face went white as the blood slowly drained away from the shock of my words.

"I'm the one who killed her, Luna. By order of the family."

She let out a strangled gasp, hands flying to cover her mouth. I pushed on, determined to confess it all, but not entirely sure why I felt the need to hurt her like this, other than that I didn't want any secrets between us. I didn't want her to hear about it from someone else who might have this information.

"I was what Luigi and your father made me. What I still am. I didn't question the order, didn't care who she was or why she had to die. I just did what I was told." I watched her, waiting for her reaction, but she just stared at me.

"She was a strong woman," I told her softly. "She was a fighter. Do you remember?"

Luna shook her head violently, tears spilling down her cheeks in rivers as she stood up and backed away from me. "No. No, it's not true," she choked out, her voice breaking on a sob.

"You know that it is. That's why I have the picture. Every person in that safe is no longer living because of me. You and Logan saw me there, standing over your mother's body. There was blood everywhere, both hers and mine. I thought I could just sneak into Gino's house, like I did when I came to see you, but somehow, she heard me. She had a knife." Beneath my shirt, my fingers found the wide, white scar that curved down around my hip. "She nearly unmanned me with that knife. Luckily, the material of my pants was tough, and she was a little off balance when she swung at me, although it did leave a wide scar."

Luna wrapped her arms around her stomach as if she could feel the cold metal slashing deep into her own skin. Silent tears streamed down her face.

"She was very hard to kill, I want you to know that. She was tough, like you. Tougher than your father is. But in the end, I was stronger than her. And I had a gun. I took my time aiming. I didn't want her to suffer. I just wanted the job to be done. You and Logan came running when you heard the shot." I paused. "I'm sorry you saw that. Both of you. I didn't know you were there, or I would've picked a different time."

"Oh, my god." Her breath came in ragged gasps and her shoulders heaved with the force of her anguish. I'd just shattered her world with my confession, destroyed everything between us. The pain and disbelief were etched clearly across her delicate features.

But she didn't scream or curse me. Instead, in a move I should've seen coming, she turned and grabbed my Glock from the nightstand. And maybe this was what I'd hoped she would do, and that's why I chose to make this confession when it was right there, within her reach. I wasn't ever careless with my weapons.

Before I could react, she swung the gun toward me, hands trembling violently, and pulled the trigger.

Fire erupted in my right side as the bullet tore through flesh and muscle, right above the scar her mother had given me. I grunted in pain, gripping my side as crimson blood seeped through my fingers. The force of the shot knocked me back a step, but I kept my feet under me through sheer force of will. I'd been shot before, but this one hurt more than most. It took me a moment to realize it was because it had come from her. The initial burst of agony slowly started to subside into a throbbing, searing ache that seemed to pulse in time with my racing heart.

Luna stared at me, and I could see the horror on her face at what she'd done. She dropped the gun on the floor. "Why?" she choked out. "Why are you telling me this?"

She remembered. I could see it on her face. Bending over carefully, I picked up the weapon, ejected the cartridge, and laid them both on the bed behind me. Easy to reload, but long enough for me to get it away from her if she tried to shoot me again. My side burned like hell, but that pain was nothing compared to the anguish in her voice. "Because you needed to know."

She backed away from me until she hit the wall near the door, then slid to the floor with her face in her hands.

I thought confessing my sins would make me feel absolved. But I felt nothing for what I'd done, only unsettled because I could see how much my actions were hurting Luna. "I'm sorry," I said hoarsely. "For what I did. For what I took from you." Strangely enough, I realized that I actually meant it. Perhaps for the first time in my life.

She didn't respond. Just kept sobbing into her hands.

I knew then that I'd lost her for good. The monster I was could never be redeemed in her eyes. She would never look at me the same way again. This thing I'd done was too terrible, my sin too grave. Confessing had only deepened the chasm between us. Luna finally saw me for what I truly was—someone capable of inflicting terrible harm without remorse. My empty apologies meant nothing to her. I was a cold, ruthless man, and I'd caused her too much pain.

There could be no going back now.

And yet, it was only after I saw all of this that I realized I'd been wrong. Whatever happened in the end, I couldn't let her go.

Picking her up off the floor, I took her into the other room. When she realized what I was about, she began to struggle, kicking and screaming and hitting me. But I only held her tighter, warm blood running into the waistband of my pants, until I got to the cell. Throwing her over my shoulder, as I'd threatened to do at Luca's, I unlocked the door and took her inside. I dropped her on the floor, closing and locking the door before she could get to her feet.

She screamed and cursed at me as I backed away until I was out of reach. I stayed, watching, until the fight drained out of her. Her hands slid down the bars until she was on her knees, her head hanging forward so I couldn't see her face.

I took a step forward, then stopped.

With one last look at the broken woman on the floor, I turned and went back to my room, grabbing my weapon and jacket from the bed. Each step sent jolts of pain lancing through my side, but it barely registered as I walked away, my throat burning with my own tears. The pain in my chest was so unbearable it made the gunshot in my side feel like little more than a scratch.

As soon as I was in the hall, I stopped and leaned against the wall, trying to gather myself into some form of the man I was before, to push down the unfamiliar feelings threatening to overwhelm me.

How did people live this way? How did they go about their day with such agony inside of them? It was too much.

I couldn't separate or name the things I was feeling, and I didn't know how to make it stop. I'd always thought emotions were a weakness, something to be crushed and discarded. But now I realized they were a force to be reckoned with, a raging inferno that could destroy everything in its path.

Destroy *me*.

I scrubbed my face with my hands, trying to clear my head. But it was no use. The floodgates had been opened, and I didn't know how to close them again. Every time I blinked, I saw Luna's face, twisted in agony and betrayal. I heard her sobs echoing in my ears, felt the weight of her pain settling on my shoulders.

I couldn't do this. I needed to make it stop. What did a normal person do when they couldn't fix their head?

Pulling out my phone, I dialed the office of a psychiatrist I'd seen plastered across every billboard in the city. His assistant answered on the second ring.

"I need an appointment," I ground out. "Now."

She started to tell me the doctor had no availability until the following month. However, once I emphasized how *urgent* this was, and that I would pay triple his normal rate, she miraculously found an opening right after lunch.

"I'm on my way." I hung up and continued down the hall, one hand pressed to my bleeding side. In the kitchen, I unbuttoned my shirt. Then I wet a towel and washed the blood from my skin as best I could before I packed the hole and slapped some gauze over it with some adhesive tape. If the bullet had gone an inch to the left, she would've missed me completely.

I didn't know if the bullet went through. Probably. Reaching behind me, I felt around, and when I pulled my hand back, there was fresh blood on my fingers. That was good. It went through. I packed it up the best I could, like I had the front. Once it was covered, I washed my hands and finished getting dressed.

Luna had every right to hate me. I was a monster, through and through. My hands were stained red from the lives I'd taken without remorse, even if it wasn't visible to the naked eye.

But the thought of losing her...

Holy fuck. It shattered something deep inside me that I thought was long dead. Underneath the brutal exterior I showed the world, she'd awakened feelings and desires I never knew were possible. Not redemption. It was way too fucking late for that. But maybe...hope. A future where light could reach even the darkest corners of my soul.

Luna's light.

The doctor would fix me, cut out this weakness, this confusion and pain...then maybe it would be better. I could go back to being the cold, unfeeling killer I was always meant to be.

Because feeling nothing had to be better than feeling this.

CHAPTER 15

Tristan

"J ohn?" the psychiatrist greeted me, using the fake name I'd provided.

I stood, buttoning my suit jacket and pulling down my shirtsleeves, then checked my cufflinks, using these few seconds to not only size up the man in the doorway as he did me, but to give myself a moment for the twinge in my side to lessen.

He smiled and extended his hand as I approached, but his eyes were wary as he took in my appearance. I knew the effect I had on people, the way I made them nervous. Like Veda. It didn't bother me, and it served me well in my profession.

I clasped his hand firmly, meeting his gaze with a guarded stare and wondering if this was a mistake. But I couldn't live this way anymore, and I was quickly losing control over my own psyche.

As I released his hand, he gestured for me to proceed him inside. Walking into the office, I scanned the room, automatically noting the placement of the furniture and the lack of a second escape route.

"Make yourself at home, John. Wherever you feel comfortable is fine."

I caught the look he gave his secretary before I instinctively chose the chair that would put my back to the wall, breathing normally through the pain as I sat down. A strategic position, one that allowed me to keep an eye on the entire room. Probably not necessary in this situation, but a habit that was hard to break, especially when I was in an unfamiliar place.

I watched as he retrieved his notebook, pen, and a tape recorder from his desk. The sight of the recorder made me pause, a flicker of unease in my chest. I didn't like the idea of my words being documented, of there being a record of my being here, fake name or not.

I hoped this guy would live up to the money I was paying him for this appointment and fucking fix me. I'd been made into what I am because it kept Luca alive. It kept *me* alive. Nothing distracted me. Nothing made me lose my focus.

Until Luna.

I had to let her go, to purge myself of this obsession before it consumed me. Before it destroyed everything I knew. And if this damn psychiatrist couldn't help me, well...

I would deal with that problem if and when it happened.

"How are you today?" he asked.

"I'm fine. Thank you."

"Do you mind if I record our session? It's only for my own use inside of this office. Have you been made aware of the doctor-patient confidentiality clause?" He set the recorder on the table.

"Yes." His secretary had shown it to me when I'd arrived for the appointment. But also, I was familiar with this particular psychiatrist, knew that he was discreet and professional and could be bought. He'd appeared in court more than once for members of the family. And if I wanted his help, I would have to trust him. To a point, at least.

I leaned back in the chair, crossing my ankle over my knee and lacing my fingers together on my lap. A deceptively casual pose, but one that I knew from previous experiences would help put him at ease.

He pressed the record button. "So, what brings you in to see me today?"

"I met a woman," I told him. It was a simple statement, but one that carried a weight I didn't know how to fully convey.

I watched as the psychiatrist's eyebrows shot up in surprise, his voice laced with incredulity. "You met...a *woman?*"

I could see the wheels turning in his head. He had to be wondering why the man sitting before him would seek his help for something as trivial as a crush. But he didn't understand. This wasn't some schoolyard infatuation. This was something far more insidious, something that threatened to unravel everything I was.

"Yes," I said simply, my voice flat and emotionless.

He cleared his throat and jotted down some notes, but I could tell he was still trying to wrap his head around the situation. "And where did you meet this girl?"

"She's a woman, not a girl," I corrected him, a flicker of annoyance in my tone. "And actually, I've known her for a while now."

"And this *woman* is the only reason you came to see me?"

I paused for a moment, considering his question. Was she the only reason? No, not entirely. But she was the catalyst, the one who had forced me to confront the cracks in my armor, the weaknesses I'd never allowed myself to acknowledge. "Yes," I said finally.

"Why is that?"

I hesitated again, the words feeling foreign on my tongue. I didn't normally talk about myself like this, and it wasn't easy for me to admit weakness, to acknowledge that something was wrong. But if I wanted his help, I would have to be honest. "Because ever since I met her, it's fucked me up in the head," I said bluntly. "And I want you to tell me how to make it stop so I can go back to the way I was before."

He leaned forward, his pen hovering over his notepad. "What do you mean, 'the way you were before?'" he asked. "Why would you want to do that? People change a little when they fall in love, John. It's completely normal."

I sighed with impatience. He didn't get it. This wasn't simply love. This was...more.

I glanced down at the Sony voice recorder on the table, watching the word "rec" flash on the small screen as I tried to think of a way to communicate to him what was at stake without giving away too much.

"You have doctor-patient confidentiality, John," he reminded me. "Nothing you say here will ever be shared outside of the two of us. Not even if they put me on the stand."

My phone vibrated in my pocket and, without thinking, I reached inside my jacket to get it, wincing at the unexpected stab of pain it caused.

The doctor's eyes followed my movements, widening slightly when the straps of my shoulder holster peeked out.

Silencing the call without looking to see who was trying to get in touch with me, I met his eyes and slid it back into my pocket. "I'm not normal. And I'm not in love. I locked her in a fucking cage."

His eyes flew to my face, and I cocked my head. I watched as the gravity of what I'd said sank in, making his eyes widen. It appeared I had his full attention now. He held up one hand, palm out, a gesture of caution. "Before you say more, I need to make sure you're clear on the confidentiality agreement. It's no longer applicable if I believe you're a danger to yourself or someone else."

Despite his warning, I could tell he was intrigued. I could see it in the way his eyes flickered over me, in the way he leaned forward slightly in his chair. He wanted to understand, to unravel the mystery of the man who sat before him.

But I wasn't here to satisfy his curiosity. I was here to regain the control that had always been my lifeline. But if he thought I was going to sit here and let him delve into the darkest parts of my soul, he was going to be disappointed.

"I would never hurt her. That's the whole fucking problem." The words came out harsher than I intended.

The psychiatrist's eyebrows shot up, surprise and something else flickering in his eyes. "But you *want* to hurt her?"

I shook my head, frustration mounting. He didn't understand. "No. I locked her up to keep *him* from hurting her."

"Okay. Okay." Leaning back in his chair again, he studied me intently. "Does she have a name?"

His efforts to trip me up were entirely too transparent. "Jane," I told him.

"How long have you kept Jane locked up?"

"A few weeks." Or had it only been days? It seemed like I'd known her forever, and yet not nearly long enough.

"And you haven't hurt her?"

"No. I told you, I can't." The words came out through gritted teeth, my jaw clenched tight.

"Are you planning to let her out?"

I paused, considering the question. I'd left her out of the cell *once* without me there and she ran off and almost got herself killed. I didn't want her in my head, but I also couldn't conceive of a world without her in it. And that was when I knew I already had the answer to his question. "No," I told him, shaking my head. "She's safer in there." At least until we found her father. Perhaps longer.

"So, what do you want from me?"

I got to my feet, unable to sit still any longer. Agitation thrummed through my veins, making my skin feel too tight and the material of my expensive clothes too coarse. I ran a hand through my hair as I paced the room, trying to put into words the turmoil that raged inside me.

"I want you to fix me," I demanded. "Undo whatever the fuck she did to make me feel all of this shit, like I need to protect her. To make me *feel* at all."

He started to say something, then nearly jumped from his chair. "You're bleeding!"

As I continued to pace, I glanced down to see the bullet wound was bleeding through the makeshift bandage I'd covered it with. But it barely mattered. My mind was too preoccupied with thoughts of Luna to pay much attention to anything else. "Yes," I said distractedly.

"Why are you bleeding?"

"Because she shot me."

He did jump out of his chair then, uncaring when his notepad fell to the floor. "What are you doing here? Why the hell didn't you go to the hospital?"

I cocked my head, confused. I'd just told him. And this was much more important than the bullet hole in my side. Besides, I'd deserved it. "I didn't want to be late for my appointment."

He stared at me in disbelief. "You need to go to the hospital." He walked to his desk and pressed the intercom. "Lydia, call an ambulance for Mr..."

Before he could finish, I drew my pistol from its holster and chambered a round, the sound echoing in the small room. I pointed the barrel directly at his face. "No ambulance."

He froze, holding up his free hand, like that would stop a bullet, and swallowed hard. "Lydia, cancel the ambulance."

"Are you sure?" she asked over the speakerphone. "Are you okay?"

"Everything's fine," he lied, his voice trembling slightly. "Why don't you go ahead and take your lunch now?" Then he disconnected the call.

I kept the gun trained on him, my finger resting lightly on the trigger. I was out of patience. "Can you fix me or not?"

"I'm sorry," he said after a pause. "But other than prescribing you something akin to a tranquilizer, there isn't anything I can do to keep you from caring about someone. It just...happens sometimes. Whether we want it to or not."

That wasn't the answer I wanted to hear.

Sweat beaded on his brow. "Look," he said. "How about you lower that weapon, and we can talk about this some more. I can help you work through these feelings you're having so they don't seem so overwhelming."

"I don't think you understand. If you can't fix me, I'll lose everything." How could I do my job now? Like this?

He spread his hands wide, holding them out in front of him. "What you're asking just isn't possible. I can't just medicate your feelings away, but if you'll just let me..."

"No," I told him. "We're done here."

"You don't have to do this. I can help you."

Reaching into my jacket pocket, I pulled out a silencer and screwed it onto the end of the barrel of my gun, glad I'd remembered to grab it from the glovebox. This was not the way I'd imagined this appointment ending, but it was always good to kill with as little noise as possible whenever you could to avoid attracting attention. "No, you can't."

"I can!"

"Nothing personal, Doc. But this was a mistake. Thank you for patronizing me, but this appointment is over." The bullet hit him right between the eyes. It was a quick death, and that was good. It would give me plenty of time to get out of the vicinity before he was discovered.

Taking out my cell phone, I called Matteo. "I'm standing in an office right now. There are cameras in the hallways, elevator and main lobby. I need you to make it so that I was never here." I gave him the address, and he assured me it would be taken care of immediately. Then I went back to the table and stopped the recorder from recording, slipping it into my inside pocket with my phone.

I left the body where it was. Without camera footage or fingerprints—which I'd been very careful not to leave anywhere in the building—the authorities would have no way to tie me to the scene.

I made my way out of the office building, keeping my head down and my pace measured. I couldn't afford to draw any attention to myself, not now.

As I stepped out onto the street, the bright sunlight momentarily blinded me. I blinked rapidly, trying to clear my vision as I walked towards my SUV. I slid into the driver's seat and started the engine.

My phone buzzed in my pocket, and I glanced at the screen. It was a text from Matteo, confirming that the footage had been taken care of. I breathed a sigh of relief, grateful for his efficiency. I thanked him and carefully pulled out into traffic.

I drove around the city for hours, barely noticing when the sun went down and the streetlights came on, my mind consumed with thoughts of Luna. Fucking hell, how I craved her. How had a simple fascination with a beautiful woman twisted itself into this?

My hands tightened on the steering wheel as I fought the urge to turn the car around, to go back to her. If there was any way to get her out of that cell other than the key in my pants pocket, I'd have Enzo release her and send her and her brother far, far away. Yet the thought of letting her go made something dark and possessive rear up inside me, so strong a low growl reverberated through my chest.

Jerking the steering wheel to the side, I pulled off into a restaurant parking lot. Luna belonged to me. Not by her choice or mine, but because of the fucked-up sense of humor of fate.

Was she hungry? Cold?

Did she miss me, despite the things I'd told her?

I closed my eyes and took a breath, and when I opened them, a sense of calm flowed through me.

Turning on my blinker, I pulled back out of the parking lot and headed toward home.

CHAPTER 16

Luna

I sat in the cell with my back pressed against the wall, staring at nothing through eyes that felt gritty and raw, the weight of Tristan's revelation crushing me like a ton of bricks.

He'd murdered my mother. Left Logan and I alone with only Gino for a father. A man who'd thrown us into the system and didn't give a shit what happened to us as long as he didn't have to look at us anymore.

Knowing the horrific details of how my mother had struggled against Tristan as he brutally ended her life made bile rise in my throat. I wanted to scream at him, to demand how he could be so cruel as to describe her desperate fight for survival to me. What kind of twisted monster would share something so sickening to that woman's child?

My mouth filled with saliva, and my stomach churned violently. I thought I might actually be sick right there on the cold concrete floor. Squeezing my eyes shut, I tried to block out the images that were now seared into my mind, but it was no use. His words echoed in my head, tormenting me with the knowledge of my mother's final, terrifying moments.

I wrapped my arms around my knees, trying to hold myself together as I began to rock back and forth on the floor mindlessly. Everywhere I looked, I saw him standing over my mother's dead body, both covered in blood. Was it my imagination? Or was I remembering now that I knew the truth?

I guess it didn't really matter.

The strange thing was, it wasn't that I didn't understand why he'd killed her. I knew it wasn't anything personal against my mother. He'd only been obeying orders, the way he'd been trained. But understanding the reason behind it didn't make the pain any less. It didn't stop this hollow ache spreading through my chest or quell the hatred rising in my throat.

It didn't stop the shattering of my heart.

The door to the bedroom opened and Tristan appeared. He'd taken off his jacket, and his white shirt was stained with blood where I'd shot him. His skin was pale and clammy and his eyes were strained with pain. My heart lurched seeing him like that, and despite everything he'd done, I was glad that I had sucky aim.

I almost laughed. God, I was sick.

He had a glass tucked in his arm and a plate in his hand. The smell of garlic and lemon quickly permeated the room.

My stomach rolled, and I swallowed hard.

"I brought you something to eat," he said, his deep, raspy voice carefully controlled as he came into the room, leaving the bedroom door open behind him.

I stared at him as he unlocked the door to the cell and set the plate and glass inside before locking me in again. How could he act like everything was normal after what he'd told me? How could he stand there and offer me food like nothing had happened? Like I hadn't just shot him?

"I'm not hungry," I said, my voice barely above a whisper.

"You need to eat, Luna," he said, his voice firm.

Rising slowly to my feet, I picked up the plate and studied the contents. A perfectly breaded and browned chicken filet lay on top of fettuccine noodles, both drizzled with the lemon sauce. Under normal circumstances, I'd already be shoveling it into my mouth.

But not today. I hurled the plate at the bars with all my strength. Food splattered everywhere, coating the cold metal and the floor, even speckling his expensive designer pants with the creamy lemon sauce. Snatching up the glass, I launched that at the bars too, feeling a twisted sense of satisfaction as it exploded into glittering shards. "I'm not hungry!" I screamed, all the anger and confusion pouring out of me in a tidal wave of emotion I could no longer contain.

He didn't so much as twitch. "I did what I had to do, Luna." He sounded tired. "It was a long time ago."

I shook my head, my long hair falling into my face and my eyes filling with tears that ran down my cheeks. "It doesn't matter how long ago it was," I said. "You took her away from me. You took away the only decent family I had."

He took a step toward me. "I'm sorry, *bambolina*," he said. "I truly am. But I can't go back and change the past."

"Don't call me that," I spat out.

I was overwhelmed by a potent mix of anger and grief that threatened to consume me. Every fiber of my being wanted to hate him. I longed to scream at him until my throat was hoarse, to claw at his face and make him feel even a fraction of the agony that was ripping me apart.

And I wanted to pull him into my arms and let him take me, possess me, make me feel something other than this god-awful pain I felt now. Anything to numb the searing anguish that consumed my heart and soul. As sick as it sounded, I was desperate to lose myself in him, even if only for a fleeting moment, just to escape the suffocating emotions that threatened to crush me.

He took a deep breath and let it out slowly, swaying on his feet. "I was a very young man. I was trying to prove myself to Luca's father, to earn his approval." He paused. "And maybe...*non lo so*," I don't know, "...maybe I wanted to hurt Gino." His dark eyes searched mine. "Everyone knew how much he loved her, even if perhaps she didn't feel quite the same way."

I could only stare at him. I knew he was telling the truth, but it didn't make it any easier to accept. "Why are you telling me this now?" I cried. "Why?" I threw my arms out to the sides, indicating the cell I was imprisoned in. "Is this a fucking game to you?"

"I told you because I want you to know the truth," he said. "I don't want there to be any secrets between us."

"There is no 'us,' Tristan."

Glass crunched under his shoes as he came closer. When he reached the bars, he wrapped his fingers around them and rested the side of his head against the cold metal, his dark eyes on me. "But there is, *bambolina*. It's only us, and that's all there will ever be. I'm beginning to see that now. There's no fighting it."

I wrapped my arms around myself. "I don't think I can ever forgive you for this," I whispered, my voice thick with fresh tears. "Not for this, Tristan." I searched his dark eyes, desperately trying to find a glimmer of remorse or regret, but there was only acceptance and an unwavering conviction.

His dark eyes met mine. "You will. Someday."

I started to deny it, to swear to him that I never would, to ask him if he planned to keep me locked up for the rest of my life, but he pushed himself off the bars.

"Where are you going? Tristan! Let me out of here!!"

I watched as he turned and staggered out of the room, closing the door behind him. The click of the latch sliding into place echoed through the space, a harsh reminder that I was still his prisoner.

Sinking back down to the floor, I buried my face in my hands as I let the tears fall. I didn't even try to hold them back, my body shaking with the force of my sobs.

I didn't even know if I was still crying for myself or because I was worried about him.

How had my life come to this? Being held captive by a man who had murdered my mother in cold blood? A man who claimed to care for me, yet had no problem locking me in a cell like an animal?

Eventually, the tears slowed and then stopped altogether. I lifted my head and swiped at my face with the back of my hand.

Rising to my feet, I moved to the small sink in the bathroom and turned on the tap, splashing cool water on my face. I avoided looking at my reflection in the mirror, knowing I must look like hell.

As I patted my face dry with a soft towel, my gaze landed on the mess I'd made. The remnants of the meal Tristan had brought me.

A wave of guilt washed over me, surprising me with its intensity. Even in the condition he was in, he made that food for me. And I'd thrown it back in his face like a spoiled child.

I shouldn't feel that way.

I should despise him.

And yet, beneath the shock and hurt and anger, there was something else. A gaping hole in my chest when I pictured him pale and bleeding, struggling to stay on his feet, injured by my own hand.

What the hell was wrong with me? How could I feel anything but hatred for this man who had destroyed my family? A man who was holding me prisoner?

But even as I asked myself the question, I knew the answer. Despite everything, despite the horrible things he'd done, I couldn't seem to stop the way I felt about him. The way my heart raced when he was near, the way my body responded to his touch.

Because no one else had ever cared about me the way that he did.

I hated myself for it. For being so weak, so twisted, that I could still want him after learning the truth. But I couldn't deny it, no matter how hard I tried.

Restless, I pushed myself to my feet and paced the small cell, careful not to walk over the broken glass with my bare feet.

I suddenly felt cold and alone. What was going to happen now? Would he keep me locked up in here forever? Would he even survive the gunshot wound I'd inflicted on him? The thought made my chest tighten with fear.

"Tristan?" I called out, my voice trembling. "Tristan, are you okay?"

I knew he couldn't hear me. The room was soundproof. But I couldn't stop myself from screaming his name over and over again. I didn't even have a phone to call for help.

The only reply was a suffocating, terrifying silence.

CHAPTER 17

Tristan

I stumbled into Luca's house, my vision blurring at the edges as I clutched my side. The fucking thing was making me bleed out slowly. I needed somebody to stitch me up and check the back. The makeshift bandage I'd hastily wrapped around my torso was soaked through with blood, and each step sent a fresh wave of agony rippling through my body.

As I passed by the kitchen on my way to Luca's office, I saw Sera and Veda sitting at the table, their eyes widening in shock as they took in my appearance.

"Holy shit." Veda leapt to her feet, her chair clattering to the floor. "Stay there. I'll get Luca," she told me as she ran out of the room.

I leaned heavily against the doorframe, trying to catch my breath. Sera started sliding a chair over to me, but I held up my hand.

"You should sit down, Tristan."

"I'm okay," I told her.

Moments later, Luca and Enzo came barreling into the kitchen, their faces etched with concern and disbelief. "What the hell happened to you?" Luca demanded, rushing to my side.

"Luna shot me."

Luca stilled, and his voice was as cold as a glacier when he said, "She did what?"

"We've got to get you to a bed," Enzo said. Unlike Luca, it was quite obvious he was angry.

But I shook my head. "I just need someone to check the wound. It's not serious, but it won't stop bleeding."

Enzo disagreed with my analysis. "That sounds pretty fucking serious to me."

"Just get the first aid kit," I told him.

"I can get it," Veda volunteered.

"Come on," Enzo went to reach for me and stopped. "Tris..."

"Where do you want me?"

He looked around. "Can you get up on the island? That way, I can reach both sides of you. Did the bullet go through?"

"I think so."

Luca still hadn't moved or said a word. I glanced over at him. "It wasn't anything I didn't deserve."

"What did you do?" Sera asked.

"I told her that I was the one who'd killed her mother."

She crossed her arms over her chest. "Yeah, well, I would've shot you, too."

A smile played around Enzo's mouth and I cocked my head at him. "What?"

"Nothing," he told me. But his eyes went to his wife.

I watched the interaction with interest, then pushed myself off the doorframe and started making my way to the island. Luca and Enzo stayed on either side of me, but didn't try to help me. With a groan of pain, I hoisted myself up onto the countertop and started unbuttoning my shirt.

"Why don't you two go check on Logan?" Luca told Veda and Sera. "Do not tell him anything about this. And if you see Lisa, please send her in here."

Veda and Sera left the room, and I gingerly shrugged out of my shirt, gritting my teeth against the pain as I carefully peeled it away from the wounds, inhaling sharply.

Enzo whistled lowly. "Another half an inch and she would've hit your bowel."

"Enzo," Luca warned, his voice tight.

I glanced over at him, noting the tension in his jaw and the fury simmering in his dark eyes. He was angry, but I couldn't tell if it was at me or at Luna. Probably both.

Lisa hurried into the kitchen, her eyes widening when she saw me. "Tristan! What happened?"

"Luna shot him," Enzo supplied helpfully.

Lisa's hand flew to her mouth. "Why would she do that?"

I remained silent, letting Enzo answer for me. "Apparently, he told her that he killed her mother."

Lisa's gaze swung to me. "And did you?"

"Yes," I told her. "A long time ago."

Luca finally spoke, his voice low and controlled. "Lisa, would you please get some towels. We need to stop the bleeding and stitch him up."

"Should I call the doctor?"

"Yes," Enzo told her from behind me. "Tell him he's lost a lot of blood, but probably didn't hit any organs."

She nodded and scurried off to retrieve the supplies. I braced my hands on the countertop, trying to breathe through the pain. Every inhale sent a fresh wave of agony rippling through my body.

Enzo moved closer, examining the wound. "Looks like it went clean through. That's good, at least." He paused. "How long have you been walking around with this?"

"I don't know. A few hours."

Lisa returned with a stack of clean towels. Luca took them from her and set them on the counter beside me before leaving again.

"This is going to hurt like a bitch," he warned me as he soaked a towel in antiseptic.

I nodded, steeling myself for the pain. Luca pressed the towel against the wound and I hissed through my teeth, my fingers digging into the countertop. He cleaned the area thoroughly, ignoring my grunts of pain.

"Hold this," he instructed, guiding my hand to press the towel against the wound. He moved around to my back, repeating the process with the exit wound.

Luca finished cleaning and dressing the wounds, and then we waited for the doctor to arrive.

"What the hell were you thinking?" he demanded, his voice low and dangerous.

I met his gaze unflinchingly. "She deserved to know the truth."

"And you thought the best way to tell her was to just blurt it out like that?"

I shrugged, instantly regretting the movement as pain lanced through my shoulder. "There's no good way to tell someone you killed their mother."

Luca dragged a hand over his face, letting out a heavy sigh. "Jesus Christ, Tristan."

I shrugged. "She needed to know."

"Perhaps she didn't," he argued.

"She did," I countered. No matter what this did to our relationship, it was better that it came from me. If she'd found out the truth months or years from now, there's no way we would ever recover from that. At least this way, I'd been honest with her.

"Where is she now?" Enzo asked quietly.

"In the cell."

"Is she all right?"

I shook my head. "I don't think so. But I didn't hurt her, if that's what you're asking. She's just...sad. And angry."

"Where is the key?" Luca asked quietly.

My eyes shot to his. "I'm not telling you."

"Luca, let him handle her," Enzo said.

"She fucking shot him."

"You touch her, and I'll sink my knife into your throat," I hissed.

He was unmoved by my threat. "She needs to know that this kind of behavior isn't acceptable."

"And you need to let me handle her. Or should I start interfering in your relationship with Veda?"

His blue eyes narrowed, but he said nothing more about it.

The doctor arrived shortly after, his brow furrowed with concern as he examined the wounds, nodding approvingly at Luca's handiwork. "You did a good job cleaning these," he said to Luca. "But you should've called me immediately," he told me. "A little longer and you'd be dead."

I waited for that news to spark something in me, but all I thought about was never seeing Luna again.

"I'll stitch this up and give you some antibiotics to prevent infection," he continued. "And you could use some blood. You've lost too much."

I nodded.

"I'll try not to touch you," he told me. "But—"

"Just do what you need to do, and do it as fast as you can."

I barely felt the needle piercing my skin over and over again. The pain was nothing compared to when he had to touch me. But I gritted my teeth and willed my heart to stop racing as I fought back the demons trying to take over my mind.

Once the doctor finished and he had me hooked up to an IV, he handed me a bottle of pills. "Take these twice a day until they're gone," he instructed. "And try to rest as much as possible. No strenuous activity for at least a week."

I nodded, setting the pills on the counter beside me and pulling my shirt back on with Enzo's help. "Thank you."

He'd just started packing up his supplies when Luca's cell phone buzzed. He pulled it out of his pocket. "Yes?"

Luca's expression darkened as he listened to whoever was on the other end of the line. "What exactly are you telling me?" he growled, his knuckles whitening as he gripped the phone tighter.

After a few tense moments, he ended the call and turned to face us, his jaw clenched. "We're under attack. The guards spotted a group of armed men approaching the property."

"Fuck," Enzo growled, already moving towards the front door. "How many?"

"At least a dozen, maybe more." Luca's gaze swung to me. "Can you fight?"

I nodded. I was already pulling out the IV needle. "Yes." I already felt a little better. And, besides, it was Gino. I knew it in my gut. He was coming for us.

And I was going to kill him.

Luca didn't look convinced, but he didn't argue. Instead, he hurried out into the great room, yelling for Veda.

"What's going on?" she asked when she heard him.

"We're under attack," Luca told her, his voice tight. "I need you and Sera to go downstairs to the shelter. Now."

"No," she told him as she rushed over to him.

"Veda, so help me god, do *not* fucking argue with me right now."

"I'm not leaving you!" she yelled back.

Ducking down, he threw his shoulder into her middle and lifted her off the ground. "Sera," he said calmly as Veda kicked and screamed. "Come with me."

She looked in Enzo's direction.

"Go on," he told her. "I'll come get you when it's over."

"You'd better," she answered. "I'm too young to be a widow." Then she ran over and kissed him hard on the lips before chasing after Luca and Veda.

In the chaos, I caught a glimpse of Logan slipping out the back door. I hesitated for a moment, and the thought crossed my mind that I should go after him. But there was someone else I needed to protect more. And there was nothing wrong with his legs. He could run. Find a place to hide.

The sound of gunfire erupted outside, and I tensed halfway across the great room. I looked over my shoulder in the direction Luca had gone, and then toward the door. Then back over my shoulder. Torn between my duty to my boss and my need to protect Luna.

I was created to protect him.

I was born to be with her.

My legs begin to move, carrying me swiftly across the room. I had no weapon. No way to defend myself. But I had to get to her.

"Tristan."

Enzo had to step in front of me to get me to stop. My upper lip lifted in a snarl. "Get out of my way."

"Here," he said. "Take this."

I looked down. He was handing me a gun.

"Bring her here and we'll get her in the safe room."

"No."

"Tristan, fucking listen to me. It's the safest place for her. You know as well as I do that's Gino out there. If he gets into your house, he can shoot through bars. Shoot through walls. She'll be safer here. Bring her HERE."

I gave him a sharp nod and he moved out of my way.

CHAPTER 18

Luna

The bedroom door opened and the rush of relief that hit me when I saw Tristan standing there made me lightheaded. He looked better, a little less pale than when he left.

Thank you.

"We need to go, Luna."

The words had barely left his lips, when suddenly, through the open bedroom door, I heard a series of sharp, distinct pops.

Pop! Pop! Pop!

The sound was unmistakable, sending a jolt of fear through my body. It was quickly followed by the rapid staccato of what sounded like an army of guns firing, the noise echoing through the house and causing my heart to race with dread. I froze, my mind reeling as I tried to process the chaos erupting around us, wondering what fresh hell awaited me now.

My eyes flew to Tristan as he stilled, listening. Without a word, he turned and rushed from the room, one hand over the hole in his side.

"Tristan!" I screamed, my voice raw with terror. There was more gunfire, the harsh blasts ripping through the air, and this time, I heard shouts—angry, frantic voices I couldn't identify. They seemed to be coming from everywhere at once, surrounding the house in a cacophony of chaos and violence.

Oh, my god. A rush of adrenaline surged through my veins, the force of it throwing me off balance. I staggered, catching myself against the wall as my heart raced wildly in my chest, pounding against my ribs like it wanted to break free and take off without me. Fear prickled along my skin, raising the fine hairs on the back of my neck and sending icy tendrils of dread slithering down my spine. I couldn't seem to catch my breath, my lungs constricting as panic clawed at my throat. What the hell was happening? Were we under attack?

Still barefoot, I ran through the mess on the floor and shook the cell door, knowing it would do no good. "Tristan!" I screamed again.

I ran into the bathroom, searching for something I could use as a weapon.

"Luna."

I froze behind the bathroom door. Tristan. It was Tristan. A sob of relief tried to escape, and I slapped my hand over my mouth. I stayed where I was. I wasn't stupid. It could be a trap. Someone could have him at gunpoint.

Someone like Gino. Because who else would be attacking us?

I heard the clink of a key in the lock and the creak of the cell door. "Luna!"

Peering through the crack between the door and the wall, I saw him. Tristan was inside the cell. He had a gun in his left hand. And he was alone.

As soon as I came out, he grabbed my arm. "Come on. We have to go."

"Where are you taking me?" I cried. Now that I was out of that room, it sounded like World War 3 was happening right outside his door. "Tristan, we can't go out there."

At the front door, he stopped and turned to face me. I sucked in a breath when I saw how dead his eyes were. The fire that always burned within them when he looked at me was gone, and I wouldn't admit to myself how much I missed it. Ignoring the chaos outside, he gently brushed my hair back from my face. "Luca has a safe room in his house. I'm taking you there."

"You told me I'd be safe here. You told me I'd be safe in your cell. You could lock us both in." I didn't know why I was arguing with him. The only thing I'd ever wanted was to be out of that fucking cell. But I couldn't let him leave again. He was in no shape to fight.

"That was before your father brought a Russian army to our doorstep." He coughed, wincing.

"We can hide here," I insisted.

But he tightened his jaw and shook his head. "It's all right. You're safe with me. I won't let anything happen to you." Taking my hand, he cracked open the door and looked around. Then he turned and grabbed my chin, forcing me to look at him. "You do not leave my side, do you understand? You stay with me. No matter what. And you do exactly as I say."

I nodded.

Opening the door wide, he pulled me outside and around the side of the house. Most of the gunfire and shouting was coming from closer to Luca's. My brother! "Logan!"

Thinking back, I would remember the way he paused before he said, "He's in the safe room with Veda."

"How do you know that?"

"Because if Luca didn't put him in there, Veda would make sure he was. A fucking bomb could blow up half the cliff and they'd be fine in that room." He glanced back at me, and his dark eyes traveled over my face. "That's where I'm taking you."

"How?" I asked him, digging in my heels. "Tristan! We won't make it!"

"We'll make it. I will keep you safe, Luna. You just have to trust me."

"She was never yours to protect, boy. And you can't *have* her."

Fear curled around my spine as my head snapped to the left to find my father standing less than thirty feet away. He was alone, and he had a pistol in his hand. It was pointed at me.

Tristan rammed into my right side, and I went down as Gino's gun went off. I landed on the ground hard, his heavy weight on top of me. I heard more shots, his body jerking as he was hit by multiple slugs.

"Nooooo!" I screamed.

"Run, Luna." Trembling with the effort it took him, Tristan roared with rage as he rose onto one knee, swinging his gun up and shooting before he collapsed to the side.

Gino staggered back, but he had a smile on his face as he watched Tristan fall.

Tristan didn't move. Blood seeped from beneath him, soaking into the dirt.

No. No no no no no. This wasn't happening.

"Tristan," I sobbed, crawling to him. I rolled him to his back, a scream building in my throat when I saw his eyes were closed and his mouth slack. "No. Tristan, no." I grabbed his shoulders and shook him. "Wake up. Please wake up." I looked around wildly, searching for someone, anyone, who could help.

But there was only my father. Behind him, fires broke out around Luca's house, illuminating him like the demon he was. He staggered toward me, tucking his gun into his pants at the small of his back. "Luna, come."

"No!" I screamed. "I'm not going anywhere with you!" Bending over Tristan, I pressed my ear to his chest, holding my breath while I listened for his heartbeat. But there was so much noise. I couldn't hear anything. "Tristan, please," I whispered. "Don't leave me. Please don't leave me."

"He's dead, Luna," Gino said. He held out a hand to me. "Your place is with me. Come home, Luna. I promise things will be better."

I raised my head, every cell in my body filled with hatred for this man. "You're nothing to me!"

Gino's eyes narrowed. "I'm your father."

"You're a fucking monster."

Grabbing Tristans's gun from his hand, pure rage welled up inside of me as I pointed it at my father and pulled the trigger, over and over, until there were no more bullets. Still, I fired. Even when he was face down on the ground and unmoving, I fired.

I kept pulling the trigger until someone grabbed my wrist and I realized I was screaming at the top of my lungs. I snapped my mouth shut, and at first, I didn't understand what was happening. Then I looked up.

"We need to go, Luni. Come on."

Logan was pulling me to my feet. "Tristan."

He glanced down at him and shook his head. "We need to go," he repeated. "It's our only chance. Luca will kill us if he finds us here with him."

In a daze, I let him pull me to my feet, and we ran through the trees to the edge of the property.

We ran until my lungs burned and my legs threatened to give out from under me. I had no idea where Logan was taking me, but at that point, I didn't care. Visions of Tristan lying on the ground echoed in my head. Because of me. Because he'd tried to protect me from my father.

He'd kept me safe. Just like he promised.

I stumbled. I'd just killed my own father. Emptied an entire clip into his body. And I felt...nothing.

Logan's grip on my hand tightened as he pulled me through the dense undergrowth along the edge of the property. Just like when I'd run from Gino the first time, I didn't feel the rocks and burs digging into my bare feet. I could hear shouts in the distance behind us, and more gunfire, but they seemed to be getting farther away with each passing second.

Finally, we got to the gate. No one was manning it, and we slipped through easily and out onto the road.

Then we kept running.

We followed the road for what felt like miles. The night air was cold around us, and yet sweat dripped down my spine. But I barely noticed. All I could feel was the gaping hole in my chest where my heart used to be.

We came to another road, and Logan stopped, breathing hard. I could tell he was in pain. "We need to stop." My voice was hoarse from screaming and crying, and at first, I didn't think he'd heard me.

"No. This way." He tugged me to the left.

A little slower now, we stuck to the side of the road, taking advantage of the darkness and hiding whenever a car went by. I didn't know if Luca would bother to look for us, but Logan was right, we shouldn't take the chance.

My body moved on autopilot, numb and disconnected from my mind as I stumbled along the dark road beside Logan. The events of the night played over and over in my head like a horror movie I couldn't turn off.

Tristan lying motionless on the ground, blood pooling beneath him. My father's cold, dead eyes staring up at the night sky. The weight of the gun in my hands as I pulled the trigger again and again.

I felt like I was no longer in my body. Like I was watching this stupid girl run barefoot down the side of the road, shivering with cold.

Tristan was dead.

The man who'd saved me only to leave me rotting in a cell, and yet somehow made me feel more alive than I ever had before...was gone. I couldn't wrap my mind around it, couldn't accept that I would never again see his dark eyes burning into mine or feel the heat of his touch on my skin.

But I should be happy. After all, this was the same man who'd killed my mother.

It was too much to process, too much to bear. I felt like I was being ripped apart from the inside out.

I wanted to scream, to cry, to rage against the cruelty of the world. But I couldn't. I was empty, hollowed out by grief and shock and a pain so deep it stole the very breath from my lungs. So I just kept moving, one foot in front of the other, letting Logan lead me further away from the carnage we'd left behind.

I didn't know where we were going. I didn't care. Nothing mattered anymore. The only thing I could feel was the aching void in my chest where Tristan had been, and the knowledge that I would never be whole again.

CHAPTER 19

Luna

Three months later

I sashayed onto the stage, my hips swaying to the pulsing beat. The lights were hot on my bare skin as I twirled around the pole, my thoughts drifting as they always did, hardly noticing the men nearest the stage waving their hard-earned cash at me.

It'd been three months since I'd seen Tristan fall right in front of me. Three months since I'd fled with Logan down that dark road and eventually to the neon lights of Vegas. We'd found a cheap one-bedroom apartment not far from the club where I worked, and Logan had just enough saved up from the money Gino was sending him to get us by until we both started working. He pulled it out of the bank as soon as we got out of the city and closed down his account, as did I. It'd been pretty lean for a while, but we'd survived, and we were happy to still be together.

Although, every once in a while, I'd catch Logan quietly looking at something on his phone with a strange expression on his face before he turned it off and shoved it in his pocket. And when I'd ask what he was looking at, he'd never tell me.

After a while, I'd stopped asking.

We thought we could disappear here in sin city, start fresh. I started dancing again, and Logan found a job waiting tables, helping out with bills until we had enough saved again so he could get back into school. I didn't lie to him this time about where I went or what I was doing to earn our rent. I didn't see the point. Not anymore. And he was right. He was a grown man. I didn't need to protect him. We protected each other. And we slowly built our new lives.

But even in the city that never sleeps, I couldn't escape the nightmares that haunted me.

The club I worked for was nice, and the manager was good to me, but I found that dancing was different for now. Before Tristan, when the men who watched me shouted lewd comments when the bouncers weren't watching, it never bothered me. Now it did. And when they offered me obscene amounts of money to strip privately for them—or more—I felt like I was doing something wrong. I felt dirty. I felt ashamed.

Because I couldn't stop thinking about *him*.

To Tristan, I wasn't some nameless stripper, a piece of meat to be consumed and forgotten. I wasn't a whore, selling my body to the highest bidder. I wasn't a replacement for a dead wife, a pale imitation of a lost love.

No, he'd seen through all that. He'd seen *me*. The real me. Luna. The girl beneath the glitter and the lies. And in doing so, he'd forced me to see him too. Not just as a bodyguard or a ruthless killer, but as a man. Someone who, against all odds, had survived horrifying things. We both had. And our twisted parts had fit together to make us whole.

He'd killed my mother.

And I'd killed my father.

Somehow, in my head, that made us even.

And now when I bared my body to strangers, the memories I lost myself in were memories of him. I didn't want to see anyone else.

With my back to the audience, I slipped out of the sequined bra I wore, leaving the G-string. As I turned back around, I scanned the crowd, as was my habit, searching for someone who would never be there.

My gaze caught on a figure in the shadows. Dark hair, dark eyes, black suit. My heart stuttered in my chest...

And then I forced myself to look away as I fought down the sudden rush of tears that hit me. Every night, I thought I saw him. Watching me intensely the way he always did. And every night my heart was crushed all over again when it wasn't him. But I had to keep my shit together. I couldn't ruin my makeup. Sad girls didn't make good tips. And I fucking needed those tips.

Forcing a smile, I dropped to my knees and crawled slowly toward the front of the stage—and the bald guy with the twenty-dollar bill.

When the song ended, I grabbed my top and my tips off the stage and let the next girl take over.

"Luna!" My manager's voice cut through the music. "You've got a private dance request in the back."

I nodded as I made my way down the side stairs and headed toward the velvet curtain that blocked off the area where we could do more than strip, if the money was right and only if we chose to.

My boss grabbed my arm as I passed. "This guy just gave me fifty thousand dollars for an hour of your time."

"What?" Surely, I didn't hear him right.

"Fifty-fucking-thousand, Luna."

Although I could hear the excitement in his voice and practically see the dollar signs in his eyes, there was an undercurrent to his tone that put me on guard. "What exactly are you expecting me to do for that money?"

"Whatever the fuck he wants, as long as you're okay with it. But listen,"—he leaned in close to me—"I'm gonna have Jack stand right outside. If you need him, you yell loud."

Jack was our largest and scariest bodyguard. Only half joking, I asked, "Who the hell do you have in there?"

"Just be careful with this one. I don't like the look in his eyes."

Great. Just what I needed. But I wasn't about to turn down fifty grand. I handed him my tip money to hold for me and moved past him.

"Yell loud!" he called after me.

I raised my hand to let him know I'd heard him and pushed aside the curtain, stepping into the dimly lit room. As my eyes adjusted to the soft lighting, I searched the room for my customer.

"Aren't you going to dance for me, *bambolina?*"

For a moment, I couldn't breathe.

It wasn't possible.

Was I finally losing my mind? I closed my eyes. If I was, I never wanted to be sane again.

"Don't do that, Luna. Don't shut me out."

My chest caved in, and my throat was thick with tears that overflowed and slid down my cheeks.

"Open your eyes."

"I don't want to," I whispered. I knew he couldn't hear me over the music, but it didn't matter, because I was going insane. He couldn't be here. He was dead. I fucking *saw* him die.

That dark spicy scent that reminded me of the forest at night filled my nose, and a mournful, keening cry rang in my ears. It took me a moment to realize it was coming from me.

"Open your beautiful fucking eyes. I want to see them."

My eyes snapped open.

The man standing in front of me was someone I never thought I'd see again. Wearing an expensive black suit with a black button-down shirt and dress shoes, he looked exactly the same. A little thinner, maybe. But so was I. I wanted to throw my arms around him and never let go. I wanted to turn my back on him and run away. Because this couldn't be happening.

"Tristan," I whispered.

Oh, my god. He was alive.

It wasn't possible. "But I saw you..." My words faded away. I couldn't make myself say it. My heart thundered in my chest as I stared at him, still unable to believe my own eyes.

I didn't know whether to laugh, cry, or scream. I wanted to touch him, to prove to myself that he was real, but I couldn't seem to make myself move. Because as much as my body ached for him, I couldn't forget all the things he'd done.

And yet I craved his touch. I craved *him*. I'd missed him so fucking much. The darkest, most twisted parts of me wanted to lose myself in him the way I had before. But I couldn't. I wouldn't.

Would I?

"Dance for me, Luna." His deep voice broke through my spiraling thoughts, and I shivered. "Now."

As if compelled by some unseen force, I found myself moving, my body responding to his softly spoken command like it always had. I turned my back to him, trying to collect myself, but it was impossible. Not when I could feel the heat of his gaze burning into my skin.

Slowly, I began to sway my hips to the music, running my hands up my sides and into my hair. I arched my back, remembering the way he used to study me, the hunger in his eyes. The way he'd touch me after, his hands and mouth consuming me until I shattered in his arms.

I wanted that again. I wanted *him* again.

I turned back around, meeting his dark gaze. In the low light, his eyes looked black, fathomless. He watched me with that predatory stillness he had, like a panther waiting to strike. And, oh god, I wanted to be his prey.

Breath catching in my throat and silent tears wetting my cheeks, I slid my hands over my breasts and down my stomach to the thin strings holding up my barely-there bottoms. I hooked my thumbs beneath the fabric, toying with it, teasing him. Daring him.

His jaw clenched, and I knew I was playing with fire. But I didn't care. I'd already been burned by him. What was one more scar? Maybe someday, I'd have so many that my pain would match his.

My pulse raced as I caught and held Tristan's dark gaze, playing the seductress, every nerve in my body attuned to him. I wanted to ask him how he'd survived, wanted to ask him so many things, but I couldn't seem to form the words. So I danced.

For him.

Slowly, I turned, putting my back to him once more. I ran my hands over my hips, my ass, knowing he watched every move I made. My blood raced, sensitizing my skin, and arousal pulsed between my thighs.

The song changed, something slower, sexier, and I matched my movements to the sensual beat. I could feel Tristan's eyes on me, lighting my skin on fire as it traveled over my body. It made me shiver, made me ache.

Suddenly, he was behind me, so close I could feel the heat of his body against my back. My breath caught in my throat, and I froze.

"Don't stop," he murmured, his breath hot against my ear. "I like watching you dance."

A whimper escaped my throat at the rough, deep sound of his voice. I began to move again, swaying from side to side. He moved with me, his body brushing against mine, making me tremble.

I wanted his hands on me. I wanted him to touch me everywhere all at once. Wanted to feel the wet heat of his mouth and the sharp nip of his teeth when he lost control. I didn't care that we were in the back of the club where anyone could walk in. I didn't care about the other girls or my manager or the bouncers. I didn't care about anything except the way Tristan made me feel.

Alive. Cherished.

Loved.

He gripped my hips, his fingers digging into my skin, and pulled my back against his front. The hard ridge of his arousal pressed against my ass, and I bit back a moan. I wanted to grind into him, but I held myself still, waiting.

His lips brushed the curve of my shoulder, making me shudder. "I've missed you, *bambolina,*" he whispered. "Have you missed me?"

A sob caught in my throat as I turned and threw myself into his arms.

He stiffened with a pained sound, but I couldn't let him go. "I thought I'd lost you," I choked out, my fingers clutching at the back of his jacket. "You were shot! So many times! I saw the blood..." I trailed off, the memories of that night hitting me full force.

At first, he just stood there with his arms hanging at his sides. Then, ever so slowly, his hands slid over my hips and around my back until I was fully embraced in his arms. He shuddered as he buried his face in my hair and breathed deep. "Shh," he murmured, his hand stroking down my back. "Don't cry. I'm here. I'll always come for you, Luna."

"I hate you," I confessed.

"I know," he whispered.

He pulled back just enough to look down at me, his hungry dark eyes searching mine. "But I won't let you go, Luna," he said roughly. "I can't."

"I thought I'd never see you again. I thought..." A sob caught in my throat. "Tristan, I thought you were dead."

He ran his hand down my arm, his fingers curling around my wrist. Lifting it to his mouth, he pressed a soft kiss to the pulse point there. "I'm not that easy to kill."

"But Gino shot you so many times. I saw it. I *felt* the bullets hit you."

"Is that why you ran from me?" His eyes flashed with something dark and possessive.

"I thought you were dead," I repeated.

"Even in death, you're mine, Luna," he growled. "You'll always be mine."

I shivered at the intensity in his voice. God help me, I believed him.

He pulled me close again, his mouth crashing down on mine in a scorching kiss, devouring me like a man starved. I melted into him, my fingers tangling in his hair as I kissed him back with all the sorrow and anger and desperation I'd felt these last few months. His tongue swept into my mouth, claiming me, consuming me, and I moaned.

My surrender was a shattering of illusions, a stripping away of the façade I'd tried to cling to since I'd met him. The truth was, in the raw, unfiltered reality of Tristan's arms, I found a twisted liberation, a dark freedom that both thrilled and consumed me.

With a shuddering sigh, I allowed his darkness to claim me.

CHAPTER 20

Tristan

"Touch me," I begged. A shiver of unease crept down my spine as soon as I said the words, but fucking hell, I wanted to feel her hands on me.

I'd stood in the shadows at the back of the club when I arrived, my eyes locked on Luna as she swayed and spun around the pole on the stage. The pulsing beats of the music had faded into the background, drowned out by the pounding of my pulse in my ears. I'd clenched my jaw so hard my teeth ached, my hands curling into fists at my sides as I watched her move, her body glistening with a light sheen of sweat under the flashing lights.

The hunger inside me had grown with every passing second, twisting and clawing at my insides like a rabid beast. I'd wanted to storm the stage, to throw her over my shoulder and carry her out of this fucking place. Away from the leering eyes of the men in the audience, their gazes crawling over her skin like filthy insects.

Everything went red, and my blood had boiled with a rage I'd never known before. It set every nerve in my body on fire. I'd wanted to rip their fucking eyes out, and still did, to make them pay for daring to look at her like that.

Luna was mine, and mine alone.

And I was hers.

For months, I'd teetered on the brink of death. And the only thing that kept me in this world was the need to know if Luna was okay, or if Gino had taken her from me too.

I couldn't die. Not yet. Not until I knew whether she'd be waiting for me.

So I'd fought, clawing my way back from the abyss with every ounce of strength left in my broken body. My recovery had been pure hell, each day an endless struggle of pain and frustration. But through it all, through the countless surgeries and agonizing physical therapy sessions, I'd clung to the memory of her like a lifeline. The thought of holding her in my arms again, of burying my face in her silky hair and breathing in her intoxicating scent, had kept me going when I wanted to give up.

Her body had never been found, and neither had her brother's. Somehow, the two of them had made it off

Luca's property. And since Gino was dead, I could only assume one of them had killed him.

Then they'd run.

As soon as I was able, I'd torn apart the city looking for her, driven by a desperate, all-consuming need to find her and bring her back to where she belonged—with me. Nothing else mattered. Not the family business, not my own well-being. Only her.

She was mine, and I would have her back at any cost. No matter what it took, no matter who I had to hurt or kill in the process. I would find her, and I would never let her go again.

It took me a few weeks, but I finally tracked her down. And now it almost didn't seem real that I finally held her in my arms again.

"Touch me," I ordered, stronger this time. I'd waited so fucking long for this.

With shaking hands, she unbuttoned the top buttons of my shirt, pushing the fabric aside to press her palms against my chest. I sucked in a breath through my teeth, the feeling once again foreign as her fingertips traced over the raised scars beneath my collarbone.

"More," I rasped.

Her cobalt eyes searched my face for a long moment, then she dropped her gaze and continued with the buttons until my shirt hung open. As she parted the fabric, her gasp resonated through the room.

"Oh, Tristan," she breathed, her voice thick with the weight of unshed tears.

With gentle urgency, I captured her hand and pressed it against the center of my chest, reveling in the burn of her touch, and allowing her to feel the steady rhythm of my heart. The bullets had left new scars to add to my collection, one last memento from Gino, and they were still fresh, but I was still here. And so was she.

I shrugged off my jacket, letting it fall forgotten onto the couch behind me. My shirt followed. As I gathered Luna in my arms once more, the sensation of her bare skin against mine was overwhelming, making my head swim and another shudder ripple through me, stronger than before. I groaned aloud, desperate to be closer even as my body revolted against the sensation.

Luna tried to pull away.

"No." *Don't let go. Don't ever let go.*

"But..."

"I just need a minute," I whispered.

She held perfectly still, giving me time to adjust to the feeling of her body against mine again. I focused on the steady rise and fall of her chest, syncing my breathing with hers, and slowly, the tension drained from my muscles and the hunger returned.

Would she ever be able to touch me without me reacting like this? I didn't know, but I hoped so, because I wanted nothing else than to have her hands on me whenever she wanted, just like this.

I'd waited for this moment for what felt like an eternity, and now that it was here, I found myself savoring the anticipation even as my body screamed at me to take her, possess her, make her mine.

Luna turned her head and pressed a kiss to a fresh scar near my heart and I sucked in a breath. Even in heels, the top of her head barely came up to my chin.

She continued to kiss each new scar, the sensation of her warm lips and wet tongue on my damaged skin both strange and exhilarating. Her tears wet my skin, and I absorbed her pain, adding it to my own. I would take it all from her. Everything she had to give. I wanted it all.

"I need you," I whispered, my voice rough with emotion.

Lifting her head, her blue eyes met mine, and I could see everything she was thinking and feeling. I waited, allowing her to make the choice. I would have her, either way, but I wanted to see what she would do.

I lowered my head and brushed my lips against the corner of her mouth. A rush went through me when I felt her tremble. "I need to be inside of you," I murmured against her mouth.

Her eyes closed, and she swayed toward me.

"Dance for me, Luna."

She still hesitated, but only for a moment. With her hands on my chest, she pushed me until the backs of my knees hit the couch and I sat, positioning her on my lap. I reached down, my fingers sliding between her thighs. She was wet and ready for me, her body trembling with anticipation. I groaned when I felt her need for me, my own body responding in kind.

Lifting onto her knees, she reached down and unfastened my slacks, sliding her hand inside my boxer briefs. Her breath caught and her eyes flashed to mine when she found me.

The feel of my cock in her small hand was... indescribable.

But I wanted to be inside of her. I *needed* to be inside of her.

Reaching down, I moved the scrap of material covering her sweet pussy and guided myself inside, feeling her wet heat tighten around me as I sank into her all the way to my balls.

She cried out, and I went still, giving her a second. But I didn't stop. I couldn't stop. Pulling her down to me, I wrapped my arms around her. "*Mine,*" I breathed against her throat.

Slowly, she started to dance.

I couldn't get enough of her. The way she moved. The way she felt. The way she tasted. I wanted to feel her come on my cock. On my mouth. Wanted to take her sweet ass. I'd been without her for too long, and now that I had her back, I was never letting her go.

Luna rode me hard, her fingers digging into my shoulders as she threw her head back and cried out my name. I groaned hearing it, my hands gripping her hips as I thrust up into her, savoring the feel of her tight heat surrounding me.

"Fuck, Tristan," she panted. Her eyes squeezed shut as she moved faster, chasing her release.

I leaned forward, capturing her nipple in my mouth as I drove deeper, harder. She cried out again, her cunt squeezing my cock as she came apart in my arms. I followed her over the edge, my own release tearing through me violently.

And when it was over, Luna collapsed on top of me, her heart pounding in time with mine. I held her, my eyes burning, so many things spinning around inside of me I felt like I would fall off the edge of the world if she wasn't there for me to hang onto.

The curtain swung back, and a large form appeared in the opening, lights flashing behind him. "Hour's up," he told me.

Pulling the small pistol from the concealed holster on my calf, I pointed it at his face. "Get out."

But he wouldn't leave without checking on Luna, and for that, I decided I would aim for his knee and not put a bullet through his skull.

"Luna?"

"I'm all right," she told him. "We're good."

When he didn't see any signs that she was lying, he said, "Call me if you need me." Then he let the curtain fall closed.

With the barrel of the pistol, I brushed her long, dark hair back over her shoulder. There were still so many things left unsaid between us, but we would have a lifetime to talk.

"You're coming home with me," I told her.

"I know," she whispered.

Laying the gun on the cushion beside me, I took her face between my hands and pulled her down for my kiss.

EPILOGUE

Tristan

Fear is my new normal. The only recognized emotion that ebbs and flows inside me at all times.

Luna refuses to see Veda's therapist, and I'm glad. I don't want her to go. If she did, they might make her realize how truly fucked up this relationship is. Then she'd leave me.

And that's what I fear the most now.

But sometimes, when the memories get to be too much for both of us, she joins me in my cell. A place where we can hide from the world and all its cruelties.

We rarely speak, and when we do it's in whispers so the demons hovering around us won't hear. We just lay in each other's arms until they fade away enough for us to rejoin life. And when Luna's demons overwhelm her, I invite them inside of me to play with mine. I can handle the darkness. I can handle whatever I need to if it will keep her in the light and allow her to smile.

But now she has shadows in her eyes from Gino—similar, if not as layered, as the ones that haunt my own. We're both damaged, broken in ways that can never be fully healed. But somehow, our jagged pieces fit together to form a whole. And when we're together, we don't have to hide the sharp edges.

Her brother, Logan, came back to Austin with us. It took some convincing from his sister, but eventually, he gave in to her. I helped him find a new apartment and get back into school. Luna tells me he'll be a good nurse, and we can always use someone with medical skills in the family.

He comes to check on his sister quite often, which I don't mind. I prefer to have someone with her who values her life as much as I do when I can't be with her. And she prefers it, too, otherwise I would insist she stay in the cell where she'll be safe until I got back. But she doesn't like to be alone in the cell.

When I *am* here, he doesn't stay very long. But before he leaves, he stares at me with distrust in his eyes, and I know the only thing keeping him from challenging my claim on his sister is the fact that he knows I wouldn't hesitate to kill him if he tried to come between us.

Luna is a part of me now, as I am of her. The bond between us so deep, so visceral, that I can scarcely imagine existing without her. She's become the air I breathe, the blood that courses through my veins. And if anyone dared to try to rip us apart, I don't know that either of us would survive the wound it would leave.

She is *mine*.

And I am hers.

I shift slightly, careful not to wake her. It's late, and we're in my bed. She's sprawled across my scarred body, the way she prefers to fall asleep. It's still hard for me to be still when she's touching so much of me, and yet I crave the feel of her skin on mine more than anything else in the world. But I don't like her so exposed, and I roll to the side, tucking her beneath me. She slides her arm around my waist and her leg between mine and she buries her face into my scarred skin, sighing contentedly.

Something swells inside my chest until I fear I won't be able to breathe, and for a moment, I just hold her.

Unable to help myself, I press a kiss to Luna's temple and she stirs slightly, mumbling something in her sleep. I tighten my arms around her, silently vowing to protect her from anything and everything that might try to take her from me or hurt her in any way.

In this life, in this world, that's the closest thing to love I can offer. And for now, it will have to be enough.

The darkness from my past never leaves me. It's what I am. And it's always there, lurking in the shadowed corners of my mind, waiting to pull me back. But I have a light in my life now. One that burns so bright it keeps the shadows at bay.

Well, most of the time.

Luna's peaceful in sleep. But sometimes, like now, I wonder how she can stand to be near me. Why she allows me to touch her. She knows the things I've done, the blood on my hands. And yet, she's here. In my arms. In my bed. Trusting me to keep her safe from the most dangerous thing that goes bump in the night.

Me.

I trace the delicate curve of her cheek with my fingertips, memorizing every detail. She's so perfect to me, sometimes it's hard for me to look at her. And I know that with time, she'll only become more so. It doesn't surprise me that she made such a good living dancing.

Something possessive and ugly tightens inside my stomach when I remember watching her on the stage. The way the men in the audience would stare at her with lust in their eyes. When I found her in that club, it was all I could do not to put a bullet into the backs of their heads. But I knew if I did that, the police would be called and I wouldn't be here now, holding this woman in my arms. So I managed to refrain. Barely.

I bury my nose in Luna's silky hair, breathing in her scent to remind myself she was here with me now, and she wouldn't be going back to those clubs. She always wears the perfume I picked out for her, and hints of ethereal florals and warm musk mingle with her own natural scent. It fills my lungs, seeping into every cell of my body until I'm drowning in her essence. That unfamiliar sensation expands within my chest once more, pressing against my ribcage.

Is this foreign feeling what others describe as love? The word feels strange, even in my own mind. I've never known such an emotion before, yet with Luna, it's the only explanation that fits.

I would give my life for her, and that, too, terrifies me.

Because love is a weakness. It's something that can be used against you. Something that can destroy you from the inside out. But it also feels like something that might heal the broken parts of me...

Someday.

She stirs in my arms, her eyelids fluttering open as she tilts up her chin and those beautiful cobalt blue eyes find mine.

A sleepy smile curves her lips. "Hey," she whispers, her voice husky with sleep.

"I didn't mean to wake you, *bambolina*," I murmur back, brushing a strand of hair from her face.

She nuzzles into my touch, and my cock reacts instantly. It doesn't matter that it was just inside of her less than two hours before. I always want her.

"What are you thinking about?" she asks, tracing the line of my jaw with her fingertips, playing with the short hairs of my beard.

I catch her hand in mine and press a kiss to her palm. "You," I answer honestly. "Always you."

The smile falls from her lips as she stares up at me. My obsession with her hasn't waned, and she knows as well as I do that what we have isn't normal. But it's what we both need.

And for now, in this moment, with her safe in my arms, it's enough.

THANK you so much for reading! Stay tuned for Milo's story...

ACKNOWLEDGMENTS

First, I'd like to thank my beta readers Isabel Jordan, Harley Stone, and Michelle Gibson for your invaluable advice on this story and for kicking my ass when I needed it. (I'm talking to you here, Harley.) I love you all!

My editors- Mackenzie at NiceGirlNaughtyEdits.com and Gail Goldie at MsSpelledWords.com. You ladies rock!

My ARC readers in Angel's Army! I love you guys!

Michelle Yenne, please don't ever stop harassing me for more books. LOL Readers like you are who I write for.

And of course, my husband for his endless encouragement, support, and tolerance of losing his wife for weeks at a time while I finish a book. I love you the mostest.

And most importantly, I'd like to give a heartfelt thanks to every one of my readers who buy my books and shout about them to other readers. You're the ones who keep me going when this job gets hard. <3

ABOUT THE AUTHOR

Hi! My name is Angel Rayne and I write dark, delicious romance with antiheroes who would burn down the world to save the woman they love. I never understood why the villains never win the girl, and so I decided to write them their own love stories where they do.

Here are a few other odds and ends about me...

-Music inspires my stories and I make playlists for every book.

-I am not a fast writer. My stories take time to write. They need to brew in my head. To have book releases close together I have to write ahead. But I would much rather take the time the stories need to be the best they can be than try to rush them out. Trust me on this one.

-I love the rain, and I'm happiest when I'm sitting in a coffee shop with my laptop as it storms outside.

-I prefer to go watch movies alone, with one of those fancy coffees hidden in my purse. (Yes, I really do this.)

-My husband calls me his "little bird" because anything that sparkles catches my eye.

-I will never have enough soft blankets. Ever.

-I love ALL THE DRAMA...but only in books.

-I will forever re-watch The Phantom of the Opera with the hope that by some miracle, this time Christine will choose the right guy.

Thank you for reading my stories, and I always love to hear from you! You can reach me at: angel@angelrayne.com

www.ingramcontent.com/pod-product-compliance
Lightning Source LLC
Chambersburg PA
CBHW031438200726

48289CB00002BA/606